Charismatic Chiaroscuro

(Poetry and Art)

Meena Chopra's art, swinging between visuals and poetry, unravels an evocative journey of a woman through 'ruins of time' and subtle life experiences. The artist's vision glides into the surreal domain of dreams while colours melt into the dynamic play of shadows. Alongside art, words become silhouettes of meaning in their concrete and abstract garb. The poet-artist unpacks mysteries and contradictions of life through images and symbols with the light effectively outlined by darkness. This book is an extraordinary coming together of bold contrasts!

— *Sukrita Paul Kumar, Indian scholar, poet , critic and an academician*

—She writes and paints about bubbles, rivers, origami, lotus, Himalayas—there can never be a simple catalogue, for each poem is unique in style and visual depiction. What resonates in haunting perpetuity is the female figure in the abstract appearing from the back— fluid, shapely, flowing from neck to trunk to limbs, yet it is impossible to isolate the body parts. — *excerpt from foreword of this book.*

—*Malashri Lal, Indian Scholar, poet, former Professor and Dean at University of Delhi.*

The subtle textures and colours that she combines beautifully with her words invite the viewer into her world of wonders. She can transform banality into eloquence with ease. Her poetry reveals subtle and astute observations of natural phenomena, from microcosmic details to sweeping macrocosmic overviews of human existence. — *excerpt from the foreword of SHE! The Restless Streak*

Charles Pachter: OC, O.Ont, Canadian Master Artist and Historian

Each piece invites readers to delve into the subtle interplay of light and shadow, uncovering the hidden nuances of our shared human experience. As a visual art practitioner and poet, Meena masterfully uses the chiaroscuro technique to reveal the volume and depth in their compositions. This collection is a testament to the power of art in illuminating the mysteries that lie within the shadows and celebrating the contrasts that define our lives.

— *Donna Child, Gallery Director and Owner at Donna Child Fine Art Gallery, Toronto, Canada*

Meena's poems have resonated for me at a deeper level. Each of her poems epitomizes what I would like to call the 'sacred feminine' – a principle that reaffirms our connection to the divine, the Goddess, the earth and each other. The poems take us on several inner journeys that are deeply personal and yet universal. —*excerpt from Generally About Books September 22, 2018*

— *Lata Pada, CM, Indian-born Canadian choreographer and Bharatanatyam dancer,Canada ,*

Meena Chopra's multimedia book *"Charismatic Chiaroscuro,"* is a unique portrait of Poetry, Digital Static, and Video Art. This book unfolds the mysteries of life, nature and Sanatan universalities. Meena Chopra has explored the vastness of her creative inner self as well as new means of digital expressions through this project.

—*Tahir Aslam Gora, Urdu poet, writer and owner of Tag TV, Canada*

Reading and viewing Meena Chopra's work is to enter a world that continues to evolve with possibilities – her creative expression is an unbounded graceful multi-media swirl.

—*E. Connie Munson Photographer & Creative Animateur*

Also by Meena Chopra

- Ignited Lines - (English)
- Subah Ka Suraj ab Mera Nahin Hai (Adieu to the Dawn) (Hindi, Urdu & Roman)
- Rang aur Noor (Colour and Radiance) Co-edited and compiled (Hindi and Urdu)
- SHE! The Restless Streak— Poetry & Art (English)
- **Shifting Sillhouettes**

 Author's Page at Amazon

 Author's Page at goodreads

Charismatic Chiaroscuro
Poetry and Art
(Poetry, Digital and Video Art)

Meena Chopra

QR Code for YouTube Playlist

https://www.youtube.com/playlist?
list=PLa4gwtdXDAY4FBJAAHEMXcaW8WKABgdF-

Through scanning the QR Codes or clicking links under the artworks for the digital copies you may watch the video art on YouTube Channel

---

Published by the Author

This book includes QR codes to enhance the reader's experience with additional content and resources. While functional at the time of publication, the availability of QR code links and their content may or may not change due to factors beyond the author's or publisher's control, such as technical issues or third-party platform changes. The author and publisher disclaim responsibility for any disruptions or non-functionality of the same.

- *Price : US $30*

- *Digital Photo frames loaded with Art Videos are available on demand.*
- *Limited-edition canvas prints with QR codes for playback are available on demand.*

Authored, designed and produced by Meena Chopra

Supported by Mississauga Arts Council's MicroGrant Program through the support of RAMA Gaming House - Charitable Gaming at City of Mississauga.

To Tia and Bhupi

Contents

Art Images: 12, 13, 14, 16, 18, 21, 23, 24, 26, 32,
34, 37, 38, 41, 42, 44, 47, 48, 51, 52, 54, 57, 59,
60, 63, 65, 66, 69, 70, 72, 75, 76, 79, 80, 83, 84,
87, 89, 90, 93, 95, 97, 99, 101, 102, 104, 107, 108,
111, 112, 114, 117, 118, 120, 122, 124, 125, 126,
129, 130, 132, 133, 135, 136, 138, 140, 143, 145,
147, 149, 151, 153, 154, 156, 158, 161, 162. 164,
170, 176

Total Art Images: 80

Total QR Codes: 78 —connecting Art Videos on
YouTube (embedded below the images and poems)

या निशा सर्वभूतानां तस्यां जागर्ति संयमी।
यस्यां जाग्रति भूतानि सा निशा पश्यतो मुनेः॥"

"The night of the wise person is illumined, the night of all beings is the day for the introspective seer."
—-*Bhagavad Gita 2.69*

In order to know the light, we must first experience the darkness.
—*Carl Jung , Psychiatrist and Psychoanalyst*

"Between light and shadow, between science and superstition, there is another dimension. A dimension of sound, a dimension of sight, a dimension of mind. You're moving into a land of both shadow and substance, of things and ideas. You've just crossed over into the Twilight Zone". —*Rod Serling, (American screenwriter and television producer)"The Twilight Zone"*

https://youtube.com/shorts/o4L8hiwz0E8

Soaring through shadows
She flutters
Entwining a deep night
Threading a Chiaroscuro—

https://youtube.com/shorts/Mpdm8rCPiIc

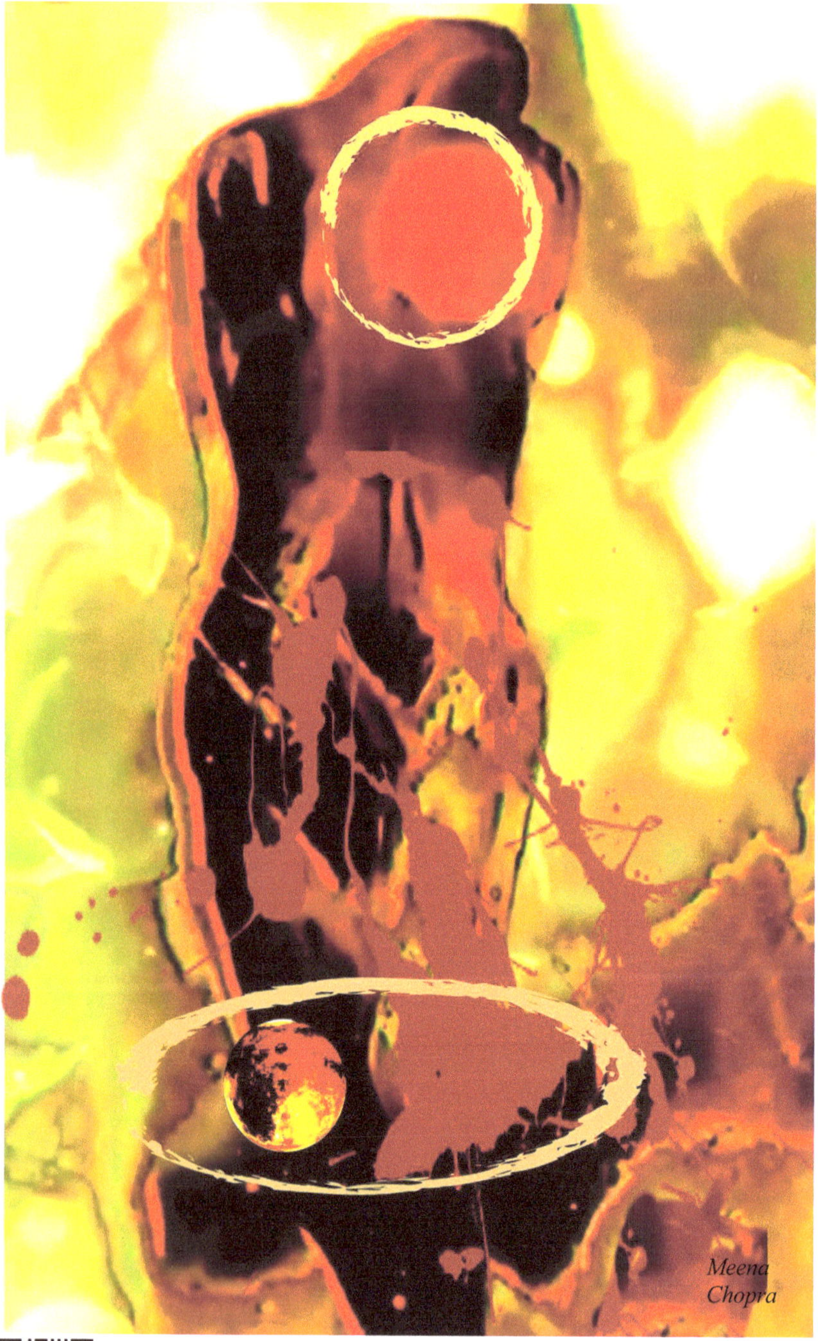

Meena
Chopra

Immersion

'Chiaroscuro' — An effect of contrasted light and shadow created by light falling unevenly. It is a technique in art characterized by the use of strong contrasts between light and dark to create a sense of volume and depth in the composition.

Charismatic Chiaroscuro—(Poetry and Art) and *Shifting Silhouettes—(Poetry)* complement each other, offering distinct yet interconnected experiences. *Shifting Silhouettes* serves as the harbinger, presenting a condensed, traditional collection of poetry designed to stir the soul and inspire introspection. In contrast, *Charismatic Chiaroscuro* builds on these themes with a multimedia approach, blending poetry, digital art, and video art to create a dynamic interplay of light, shadow, tradition, and innovation. QR codes link print to immersive visual experiences, transforming the extended edition into a layered, luminous, inter-sensory journey. Together, these books explore creativity's spectrum—from the simplicity of words to the richness of multimedia expression.

I extend my heartfelt gratitude to Prof. Malashri Lal for her dedicated engagement with these two complementary books, despite her many commitments. Her insightful and thorough foreword adds immeasurable depth to these works, and I am truly honoured by her contribution.

Meena Chopra

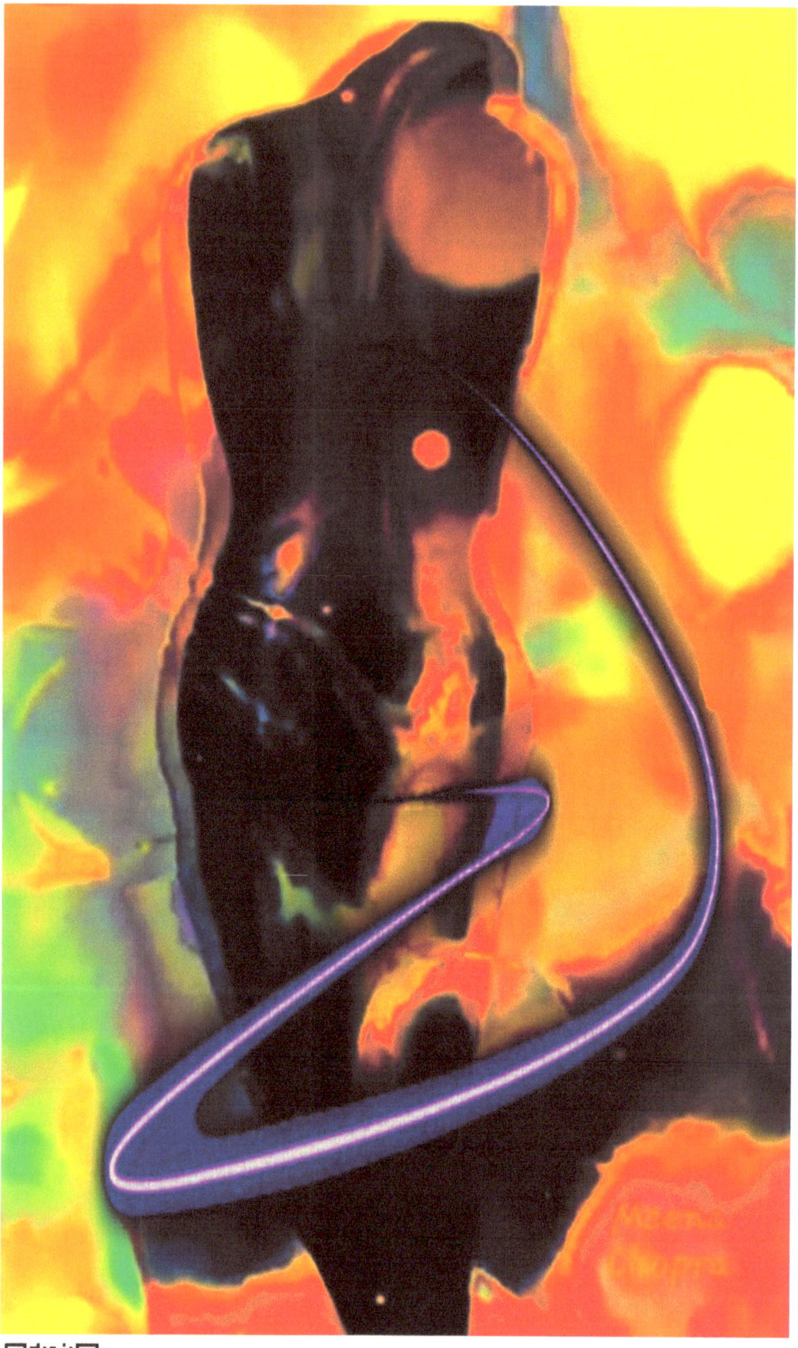

Yearnings Entwined

https://youtu.be/DEwZ2HaF03I

Meena Chopra
Poetic Pirouettes and the Art of Plenitude
By Malashri Lal

Sometimes one is dazzled by the virtuosity of Meena Chopra, sometimes one is frozen into a mesmerized onlooker as poetry, sculpture, digital movements and the dance of colours interweave through the collection titled *Charismatic Chiaroscuro*. At a certain level, this has the thrill of interstellar travel where no one has ventured before, at another level, it is the mind-travel of a Himalayan ascetic whose breathing speaks to the cosmos. The range is spectacular, the artistry amazing, and the technological innovations captivating. Meena Chopra reveals in the Introduction, *"It's a cyclical relationship that mirrors the complicatedness of the deep-rooted subjectivity of life. I would like to mention here that when these subtle experiences come to the fore, they inherently infuse a degree of abstraction into my verses and artworks because of their natural subjectivity and subtleties."*

Given this encounter with Meena Chopra's poetic pirouettes, which moments should I hold for a poised reflection? Predictably perhaps, I will pause at the mythologies, a remarkable disquisition on universal creation through the triptych of *Brahma, Vishnu, Mahesh,* but the concept is not limited to religious practitioners. The beauty of a diaspora consciousness is its transitions and interrelatedness with other cultures and an integration of essential concepts that are, after all, common to all human kind. Hence, creation, sustainability and destruction are an eternal cycle everywhere. When Meena Chopra finds this etched in the rocks of Arizona, a staggering zone of majestic landscape, I stand admiring her inspired words, accompanied by a fluid painting in contrasting colours:

Realities and yearnings entwined
legends buried in stones
engraving narratives
The truths of a Mythical Chronology
carved on the rocky riverside.
(A Mythical Chronology)

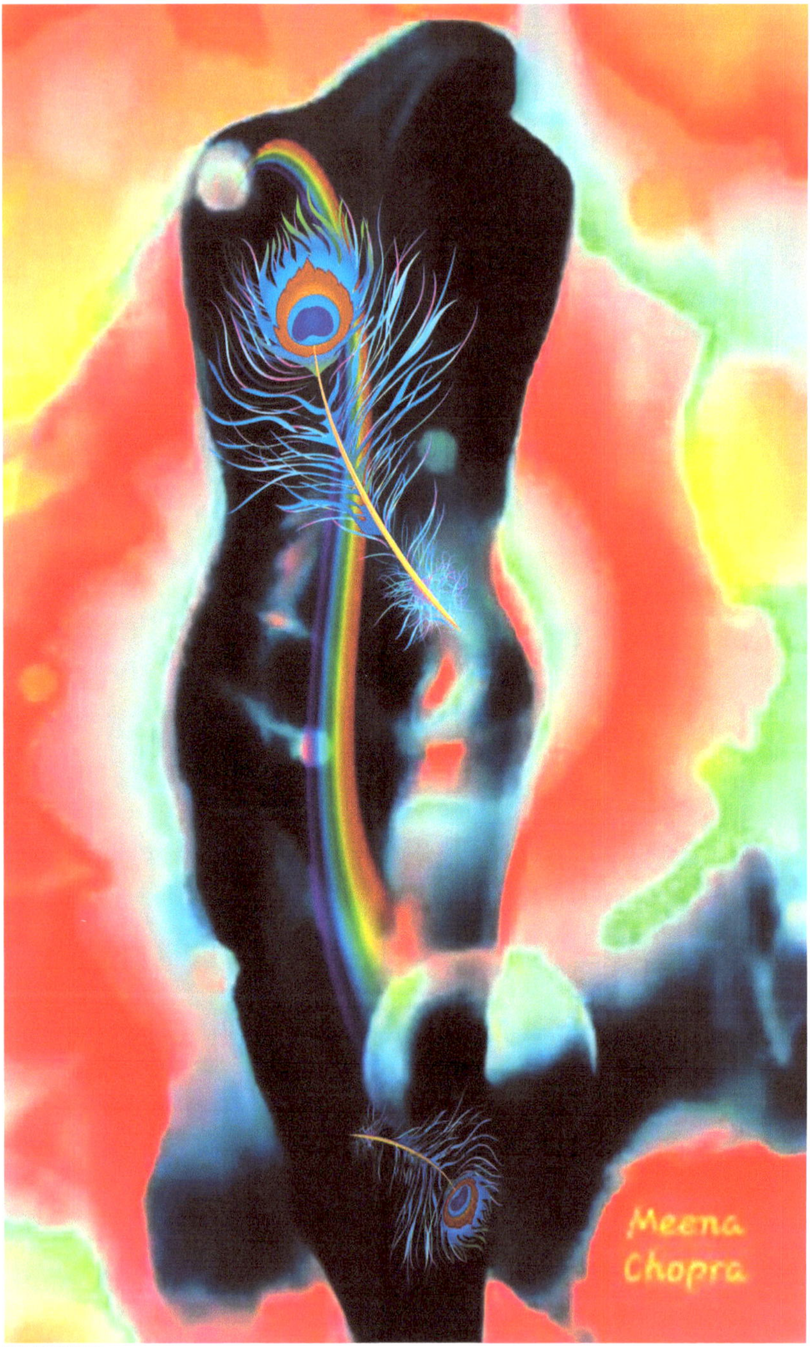

A Vivid Spectrum

https://youtu.be/pSmEZkRfnWM

The cosmic dance is around and within us, says all philosophy. Meena demonstrates the conjoined inner and outer aporias in several poems of which I choose only one here, *"Chiaroscuro Ballet"*:

Crimson whirlwind spins
a draft undulates in the vortex
currents meander
a ceaseless flux of landscapes
passes through me

What is chiaroscuro in the artist's language since the concept reverberates throughout the collection? Of the many definitions possible, this one is chosen by Meena: *"Chiaroscuro is a technique in art characterized by the use of strong contrasts between light and dark to create a sense of volume and depth in the composition."* I'd like to elaborate on this description from my perspective. The constant shift, the movements and mergers between light and dark in Meena's work fascinate me, as in the poem I have cited. It's a truism to say that each moment is never repeated. Yet the human memory holds on to some, playing it repeatedly for its emotional content of joy or sorrow, terror or ecstasy. Meena's poem, *"The Deep Dark Woods"*, (reminiscent of Robert Frost) reflects every pilgrim's story, yet this one is personalized into a sensitive, lonely encounter of the self:

Silent dusk descends
in-tune with nature's rhythm.
shadows haunt
elongated on desolate ebony walls

The *painting** on the side of the poem Deep Dark Wood, is spectacular. Shades of pink, whiffs of smoke, engulfing tentacles of dark brown swirling around a figure, a rope in one corner— (why?), a black band like a gash across the back (is it physical hurt?), and three concentric circles (angels of liberation?). The poem speculates about "shadows", but the painting might offer an alternate story. The cross-referencing is the remarkable achievement of this volume. And the readers can never reach a

*P48

19

'truth'—no one can, because these are no final answers to the paradox of suffering, the mystical attraction of the dark woods, the Indian philosophy of *Vanaprasth**.

Abstract art is Meena Chopra's forte—she writes and paints about bubbles, rivers, origami, lotus, Himalayas—there can never be a simple catalogue, for each poem is unique in style and visual depiction. What resonates in haunting perpetuity is the female figure in the abstract appearing from the back- fluid, shapely, flowing from neck to trunk to limbs, yet it is impossible to isolate the body parts. This, to my reckoning, is Meena Chopra's "Unitary Woman", the "SHE" who has been the poet's subject of exploration for decades. The generic Woman belongs to all times and all cultures. And Meena keeps her eternally in mobility, change, shapeshifting through the magic of her digital art. SHE is shape and colour, body and soul, word and silence. But SHE never front-faces you because she would rather remain unidentified. As Meena Chopra's revolving, evolving, dissolving woman turns within the gyres of colour-coding with a poem by her side—the relationship of image, word, and text merge into an enchanting design. She is Now, She is Then, She is Forever. In Meena's captivating words:

Kiss me with a mouthful of eternity
raid me, shred the vizard apart
mould me with clayful reality
*seed me with coarse fertili*ty

I am deeply touched that Meena Chopra gave me the opportunity to express my thoughts about this magnificent collection, *Charismatic Chiaroscuro*. It ends with a touching poem about poets generously sharing words 'Under the Pilkhan Tree' in our garden. Once every few months, sometimes Meena Chopra is with us in New Delhi, we sit under the canopy of an ancient and bearded old fig tree which forgets to trim its tendrils. Poets meet with their new writing endorsing a timeless bond of words, friendship and care which is best expressed in Meena's touching tribute to the fellowship of poetry.

*P167

Meena
Chopra

21

As the time passed
words revolved, condensed and spiraled
climbing high, reaching the dense crown
to be cured and dried
imbibed and nurtured in the sap
preserved in the wood of the knobby trunk
protected by the bark
silver-washed for ages to come.

Thank you, Meena Chopra, for trusting the perpetuity of poetry, painting and the creative arts. May this beautiful book/ exhibition forever offer homage to the magnificence of living, with empathy.

Malashri Lal is a distinguished Indian scholar, retired as Professor and Dean at the University of Delhi, India. She is a renowned academic feminist, mythologist, and creative writer with 21 books to her credit.

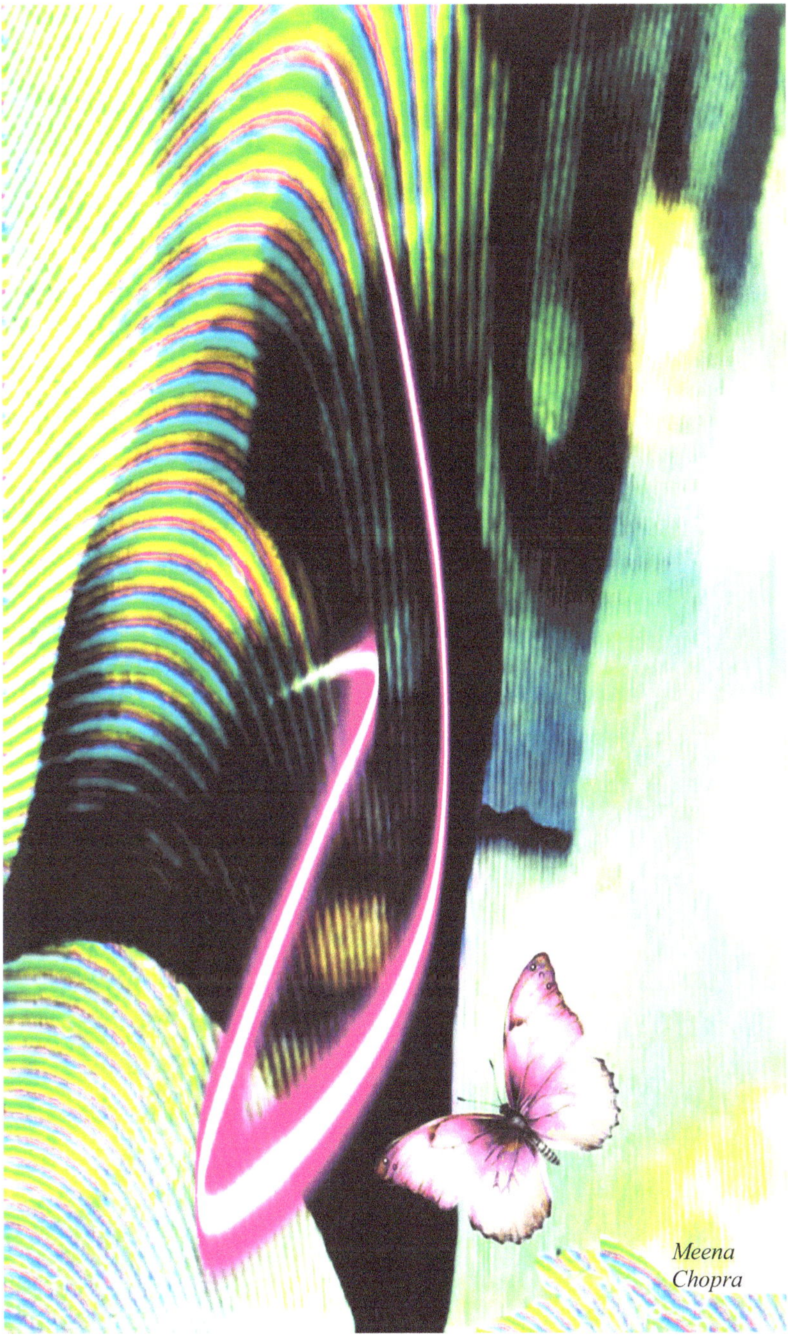

*Meena
Chopra*

Swaying Lines

She pivots, retraced—shadows lead her to the roots—
silence speaks within.

https://youtu.be/iy7cmenPKhQ

*"Poetry is an echo, asking a shadow to dance." – Carl Sandburg,
American poet and biographer*

A journey into a Charismatic Chiaroscuro—
(44 Poems , 80 Art Images, 78 Art Video Films through QR codes)

My artistic essence spans the nuances of the beauty of nature, ancient
past, age old lures, mythology, and traditions, transcending the
annals of human history. I also have a deep fascination with
the new, the modern, and the fast moving and ever evolving
world of innovations. I find joy in exploring the interplay of
light and darkness, whether in the context of celestial mysteries
or contemporary landscapes. My creativity in its abstract
expressions, and the mediums, that thrive on blurring the
boundaries, that divide the old and the new, traditional and
modern, myth and reality. Always revolving around the static
and the dynamic forces of life

A large number of poems within this edition draw their inspiration
from both my static and dynamic digital artworks. Some are
inspired by subtle life experiences of the past few years.
Featured images have a QR code for hard copies and a link
below for soft copies to watch the art video films providing a
multidimensional comprehensive and interactive experience to
the readers. By scanning these codes with the device, the

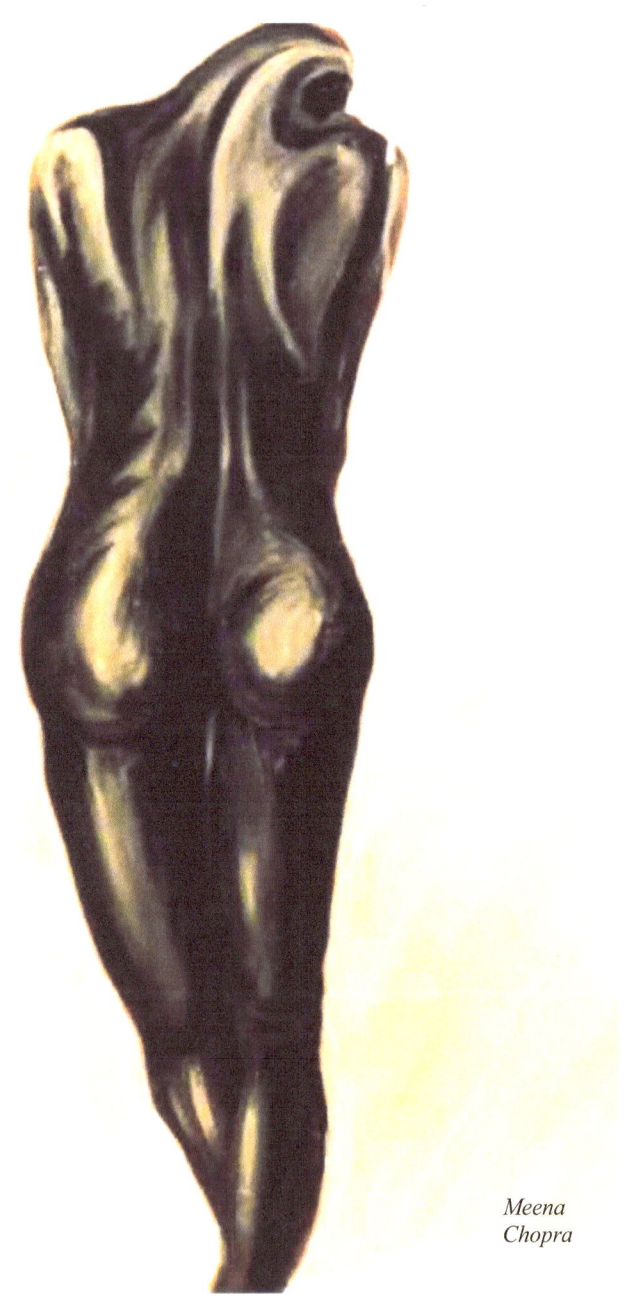

*Meena
Chopra*

Originally created in 1987, my oil on canvas piece *Reflection* was exhibited that year at Gallery Aurobindo in New Delhi, India. This artwork became a source of inspiration, evolving over time into digital forms, often accompanied by poetry, to explore new dimensions of expression.

reader will be transported into the world of video art, enhancing the engagement with words and visuals. With the exception of a few pieces, the majority of the digital art in this collection originates from my original oil on canvas artwork crafted in 1987 which was showcased in my second solo exhibition at Gallery Aurobindo, New Delhi, in 1988. Through digital manipulation, these pieces blend tradition with innovation, reimagining and revitalizing the essence of the earlier artwork. This convergence of the past and present showcases the evolving nature of art, offering a fresh perspective on timeless themes and emotions encapsulated in the original canvas.

In April 2023, during a meeting with Prof. Sukrita Paul Kumar, a distinguished Indian literary scholar and poet, she proposed an intriguing idea: to create poetry inspired by my paintings. Initially skeptical, I had always kept a clear boundary between my roles as a visual artist and a poet. However, I took the leap, finding inspiration in the individual elements of my paintings rather than directly describing them. The resulting poetry formed a symbiotic relationship between my two artistic expressions while maintaining their individualities, sparking a new creative journey. Prof. Kumar's insightful suggestion opened up new artistic possibilities for me. It's worth noting that Prof. Kumar is also an accomplished instinctive visual artist.

When I reminisce, I've always been intrigued by shadows, starting from my early years in Nainital, a quaint hill resort at the base of the magnificent Himalayan Range in India. I remember being spellbound and thrilled watching the vanishing shadows transform into various forms and shapes as the sun ascended or descended. These were the silhouettes of trees, shrubs, hills, and houses on the slopes. Particularly, I was mesmerized by the shadows of the hills and mountains cast on the tranquil Naini Lake, nestled in the heart of the town. Little did I realize that this natural phenomenon of *'Charismatic Chiaroscuro'* would play a profound role in shaping me and my creative being. As a visual art practitioner and also simultaneously delving into poetic practices, I have always felt that darkness imparts dimension and definition to light, while light bestows depth and clarity to darkness. These bold contrasts, when rippling through the entirety of the life cycle, reveal a multitude of shades, hues, and nuances that hold the essence of life itself. These life vignettes are ready to be explored and unraveled.

Life's canvas, like any artwork, relies on the interplay between negative and positive spaces to realize its meaning. I try to accomplish this through the intricate interplay of verses, digital static art, and video art in my journey through the 'Charismatic Chiaroscuro'. It's a cyclical relationship that mirrors the complicatedness of the deep-rooted subjectivity of life. I would like to mention here that when these subtle experiences come to the fore, they inherently infuse a degree of abstraction into my verses and artworks because of their natural subjectivity and subtleties.

A constant digging into the self goes on subconsciously and spontaneously. Both art practices blend with many lifelong influences and experiences to bring out a sort of hybridizing of my artistic practices, perhaps to a part of my personality too. These are immersive nomadic moments, multisensory in nature, derivatives of words and pixels that create verses, static and video images. All wrapped in an exploration and engagement of a shadow play, trying to synthesize, metaphorically, the expression of multiplicity in different artistic genres. They unwittingly embrace the bold contrasts, for it is in their juxtaposition and homogeneity that life pulsates. They become a portal to my inner world. Shadows speak to me, whispering secrets that a listening heart can decode. Their mystery envelops my world, offering solace in their depths. Art has been both diagnostic and remedy in my life's journey, guiding me through moments of joy and sorrow.

True healing requires confronting darkness and allowing it to coexist with light. I feel art's fundamental role is to illuminate what hides in shadows and reconcile with it.

This holds true for the well-being of nations, generations, civilizations, and humanity.

The digital and video art came out through a playful exploration, using apps like Gimp and VSDC on my laptop and some random ones on my phone with hours of concentrated contemplation, giving me a kind of aesthetic ecstasy. And then words started finding their way into the colours and forms and became poems. Sometimes it was the other way round when colours and forms flowed out of the words and the paintings were created. I loved this most intimate embryonic process which at times overwhelmingly elevated me beyond myself, at other times grounded me into deep detachment. The lines between these moments often blurred, with the entire creative journey, flowing seamlessly together.

I am delighted to present this intimate, multimedia, and multidimensional collection of poetry and digital art to all of you. I invite you to share and embark on this introspective voyage, explore and immerse yourself in the interplay of light and shade, and discover the hidden depths of our shared human experience within the pages of *'Charismatic Chiaroscuro.'*

As a bilingual poet, I'm excited to share that I have plans to release the Hindi adaptation of a similar collection shortly with some differences. This endeavor aims to make the essence of *'Charismatic Chiaroscuro'* (झिलमिल परछाइयां - *Jhilmil Pachaiyan*) accessible to a wider audience and to further bridge the gap between languages, allowing the beauty of the poetry and art to resonate with Hindi-speaking readers. It's a step towards embracing the richness of multilingual artistic expression, and I'm eagerly looking forward to bringing this new facet of the collection to life.

—Meena Chopra

Gratitude and acknowledgments:

I would like to extend my deepest gratitude to my cherished friends, whose unwavering support has been a source of strength throughout the entire process of writing and compiling this book. Their insightful feedback, thoughtful encouragement, and genuine belief in my work have been instrumental at every stage of this creative journey. Whether through conversations that sparked new ideas, suggestions that helped refine my vision, or simply the reassurance that comes from knowing I wasn't walking this path alone, their contributions have been invaluable.

In moments of doubt or creative fatigue, their words uplifted me, reminding me of the importance of perseverance and the power of collaboration. The countless hours they spent reading drafts, offering suggestions, and discussing ideas have helped shape this book into what it has become today. Their presence in my life has not only enhanced my work but has also enriched my creative spirit, and for that, I am profoundly thankful.

To each of you, I offer my heartfelt appreciation—this book is as much a reflection of your support as it is of my own voice.

Prof Malashri Lal: Indian scholar, former Professor and Dean at the University of Delhi, India

Prof Sukrita Paul Kumar: Indian scholar, poet , critic and an academician

Yogesh Patel: MBE, Publisher, Skylark Publications UK,Poet & Author

Naresh Kapuria: Indian Painter, sculptor, installation artist, designer, producer and curator . Director—Art Junction, Lalit Hotel.

Tahir Aslam Gora and Haleema Sadia: Tag TV, Canadian South Asian Literary Fest

Lesley Fletcher: Executive Director and Nic Brewer: Administrative Director along with the team of 'League of Canadian Poets'

Donna Child: Gallery Director and Owner at Donna Child Fine Art Gallery, Toronto.

Anita Nahal: Author, Poet and Historian, USA

Dr Sunil and Dr. Sangeeta Sharma: Editors Setu Magazine published from USA

Fellow writers at The Courtney Park Writers Group, Canada and the Chair Mary Ellen Koroscil

Fellow writers at *Poetry and You* who gather under the *Pilkhan Tree for Readings*, coordinated and conducted by Prof, Malashri Lal and Prof. Alka Tyagi

Bhupinder Virdi: My life partner

Tia Virdi: My daughter, constantly inspiring and upgrading me.

My heartfelt gratitude to the Indian High Commission in Ottawa and the Indian Consulate in Toronto for their steadfast support and encouragement of literature, arts, and culture in Canada.

Endless gratitude to Mike Douglas, Executive Director 'Mississauga Arts Council' and the team for fueling creativity with their unwavering support and vibrant energy.

Digital Nomad: Triptych of Time

In between the digital lines my breath
an endless thread
sways, sweeps, circulates.

Meena Chopra

Digital Nomad

https://youtu.be/2O72-a1D-ik

34

I am a nomad. travelling through ages
gravity anchors me firmly to the ground .
desires weave my existing *karmas**.

Destiny through ages
reflecting the trinity
Past, Present and Future

Meena
Chopra

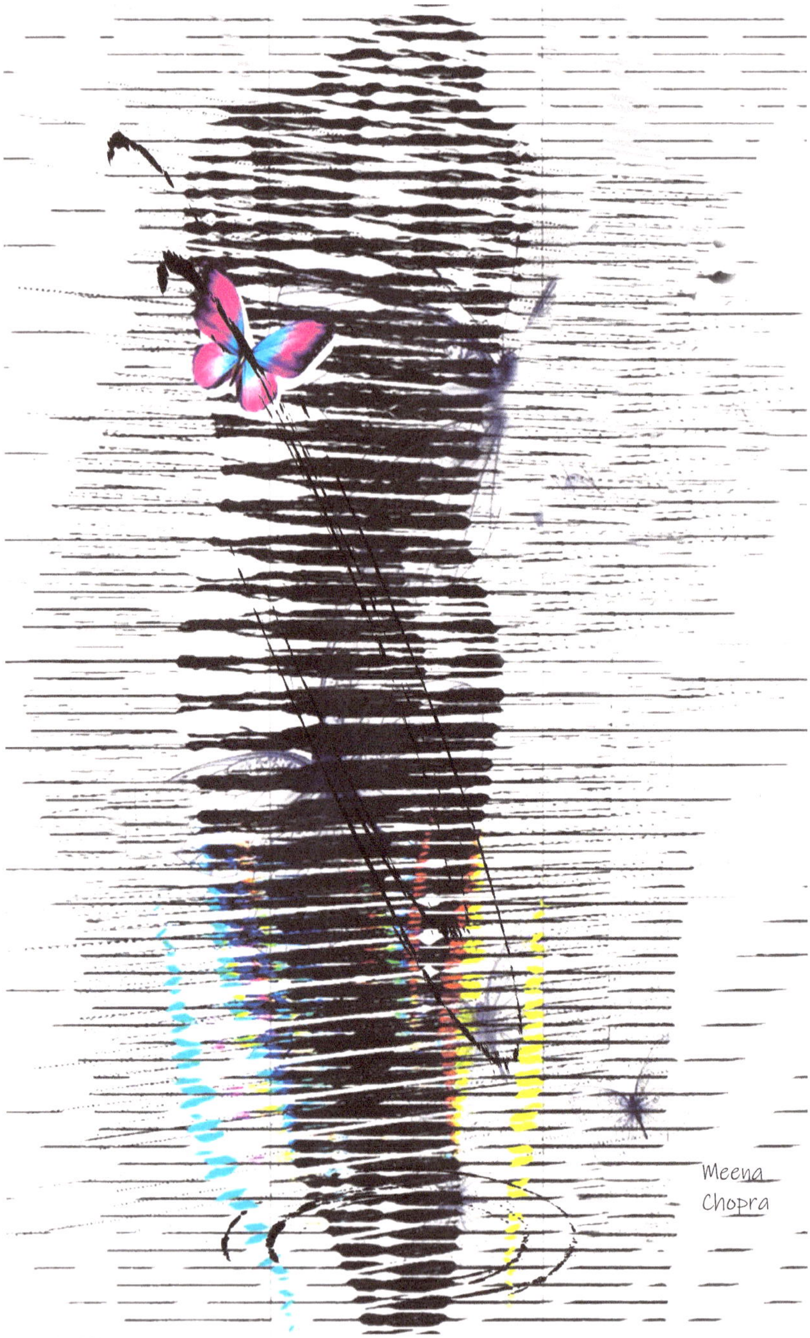

Meena
Chopra

Memories in Digits

*Brahma, Vishnu Mahesh—**
A muted trilogy
ciphered in digited spaces
Triptych of Time!

*[P165](#)

https://youtu.be/oiW9B4SdIHE

Charismatic Chiaroscuro by Meena Chopra

Silver Moments on Canadian Rockies

I inhale the mist
rising from the glaciers
where fog veils mountains
beyond turquoise waters
exhaling sultry dreams, relinquished
brewed in melting desires
on the shores of this stunning lake.
My vision calm
drifting over the fading droplets.

Engulfed in icy blue hues
I become a pebble
rippling along the velvety waters
crystal clear.

Many rivulets flow through me
draped in silver-gray
ascending into a stainless sky.

Charismatic Chiaroscuro by Meena Chopra

Meena
Chopra

Meena
Chopra

https://youtu.be/4qYPboP9vnU

A Mythical Chronology

Reminiscences ripple
wrinkling along
a shrinking river
escaping time's clasp.

A raging stream cuts through
the rough, jagged red rocks
and majestic mountain peaks.
An upheaval looms
striking my hidden existence.

Currents extinct
flowing tales of natives
Arizona's rugged edges—
hewn by time
etching canyons upon me
Running through my crimson veins.

Realities and yearnings entwined
legends buried in stones
engraving narratives
The truths of a Mythical Chronology
carved on the rocky riverside.

https://youtu.be/EzOIwcYG0OA

Charismatic Chiaroscuro by Meena Chopra

Meena
Chopra

https://youtu.be/-jP5V-Hq4JI

Rain Waters were Never Shallow

A smog-laden morning
air, thick with hues of indigo
clings to the earth
delightfully hiding
behind the overzealous clouds
silver lined with frailing moonbeam.

Tremulous dawn echoed with a calm twitter
rain dribbled from the eaves
on the desolate wings of a bird
nestled in my patio
joyous droplets glistened
dancing in my courtyard.

Each chirping echoes my heartbeat
I open the door, stepping into ankle-deep water
a shallow wet field, unfolding before me.

The drenched sun sizzles
stumbles down through the sky window
descending into the empty room, fleetingly
then rebounds to the sky, where it belonged
leaving slight traces of wet footprints
while I remained away
saturated, ankles deep in water.

My eyes shut
squeezing the joy
as raindrops tiptoe on my skin
a mustiness deep in my damp heart.

The bird flew away with
wings heavy and soaked
and joyous droplets
glistening in eyes.

Rain waters were never shallow.

Meena
Chopra

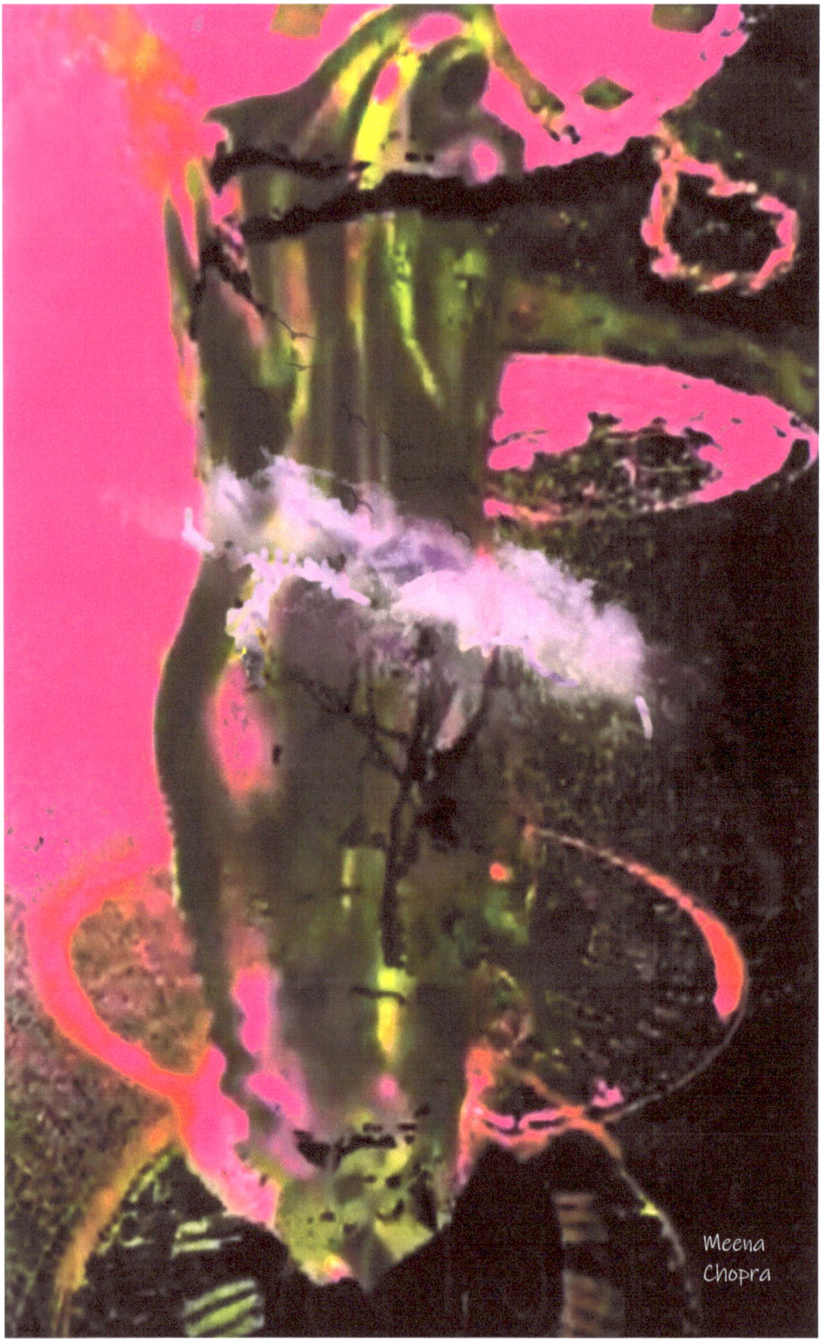

https://youtube.com/shorts/3sB3ToN2bz0

*P19

The Deep Dark Woods

She meanders on Cobalt moons
waning stars of aging regions
navigating icy glaciers
wandering in lush valleys
roaming through serpentine pathways
in a land unknown, mysterious and estranged
traversing through an untamed wilderness.
Deep, dark woods
engulfed in her eyes.

Divided, she pivots around
retracing her steps, following the echoes
back to the roots of her homeland.
She returns, nestled in safety and shelter.

Sitting on the moss-covered doorsteps
at the entrance of her home
thoughtful, eyes half closed
squeezing the sunset.
her face lights up
a gentle escape from the world of noises.

Silent dusk descends
in-tune with nature's rhythm.
Shadows haunt
elongated on desolate ebony walls.

*Artwork on the side has A digitally enhanced artistic rendition of
my grandfather's pocket watch, dating back to the year 1900*

Charismatic Chiaroscuro by Meena Chopra

A distant sun sends a lone beam
tenderly caressing the threshold
penetrating her flesh, embracing bones
delving into her being.

And then
the fading sun-rays, captured in her gaze
twitch and quiver.
infused with zeal
brimming with vitality.

A spirit renewed, leading boldly
bare and unshielded, exposed
whirls, exults, and revels
on the stage of the veiled dusk.

Countless days ablaze in twilight's zone
sliding down her body frame
illuminating silhouettes of skin and bones.

Undeterred, unfazed
she turns to the beckoning shadows
leading to the baffling wilderness
onto an untrodden trail.

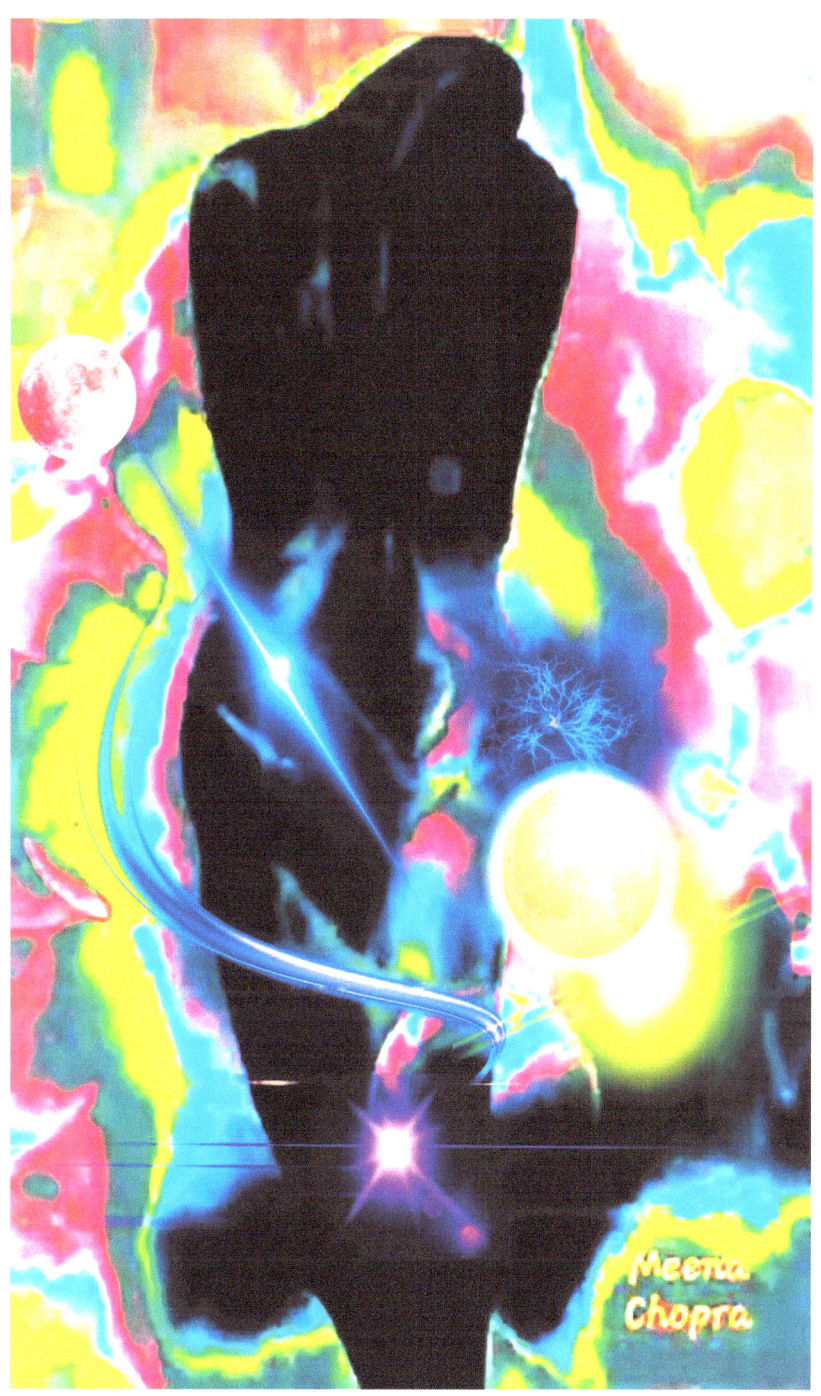

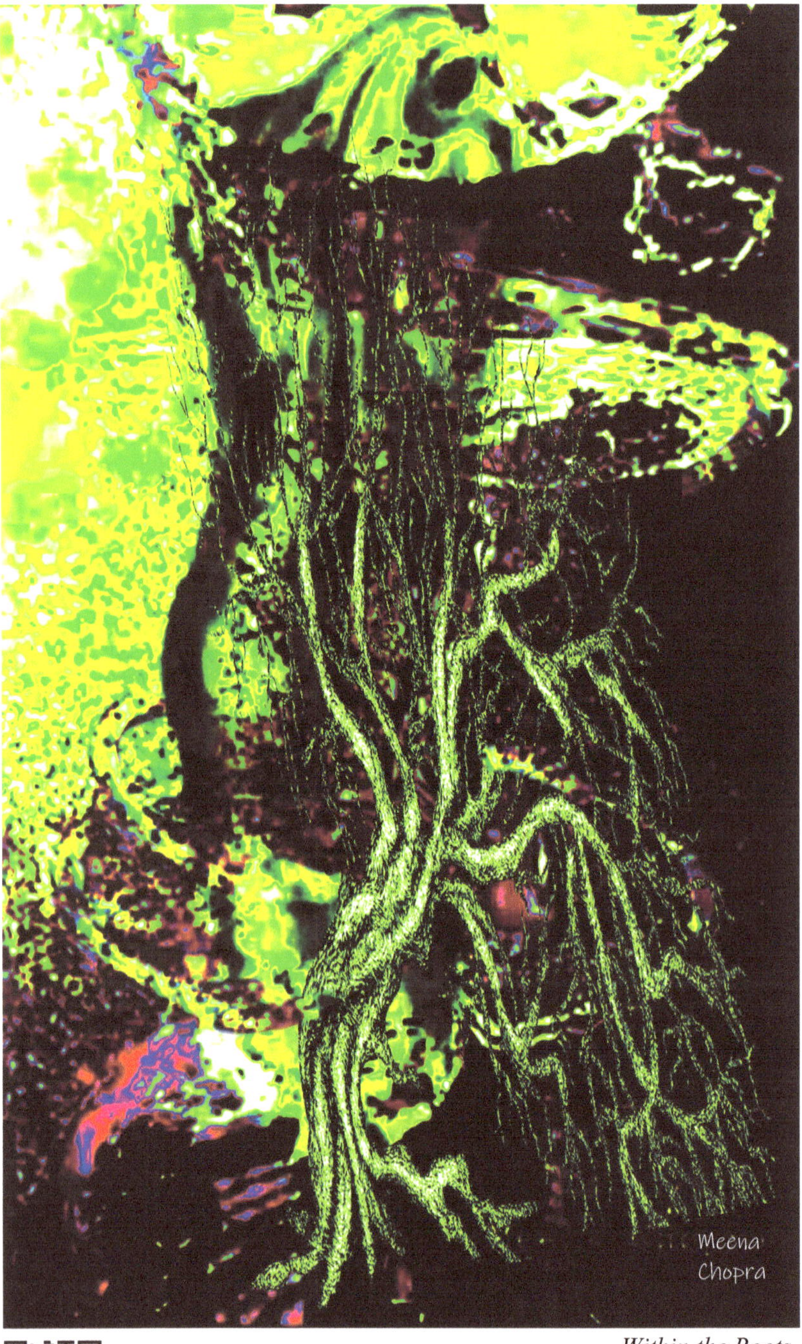

Within the Roots

https://youtube.com/shorts/ZeZTojfjBvI

She strides forth again
prepared for a new journey
ready to venture into an uncharted terrain.

Moments, seasons and years pass by
The deep dark woods
afire in her eyes
igniting endless days and nights.

The deep dark woods
mystify her eyes.

https://youtu.be/ospmAcqD30g

Ruins of Time

Barefoot, I traverse
on the ruins of time
past crumbles underneath.

Images emerge
from the wrinkled stony walls.
Ruins of *Mandu**
awaken in my wavering eyes
rippling, grooving.
cracking before me
as I sink—
deep into the past.
Legends decipher
cryptic illusions
enriched with historic reality.

Silver anklets, a soft tinkling
receding footsteps
of the poetess *Rani Roopmati**
immersed in a fading love song
echoing forever
lilting shadows sway
on the decaying walls of her palace
amidst the rubble of a timeless zone.

Charismatic Chiaroscuro by Meena Chopra

*P167

Chiaroscuro Ballet

Haunting music
a chiaroscuro ballet swirls
echoing an eerie serenade.

A sinuous wisp of smoke
rises beneath to above
finding its way to the sky
tainted with elapsed dreams.

Daylight crumbles
impressions implode
giving birth to fragmented tints
a deepening night.

Crimson whirlwind spins
a draft undulates in the vortex
currents meander
a rampant flux of landscapes
passes through me.

Lightning strikes the rootstocks
earth convulses
tremors ripple everywhere
spirits rearrange
rhizomes shootout
seeking new horizons.

Spectral shadows, an ethereal legion
slithering from murky tunnels
creep out on safer grounds
deserting their secret vaults.

https://youtube.com/shorts/YVzl35sO-zs

Choked voices
falling and melting
liquid bubbles fizzing
trapped in pitted shadows
froth spilling from the crooked edges
staining the earth
blood-curdling
darkness deepens.

A chill grips my spine
my heart pounds in the ominous silence
seeking stability.

Fluffy clouds cross the moon
a shooting star
rushes to the ground
a tinge of hope
breaking the darkness
A gentle touch in these raging times.

Written at the beginning of the Gaza war, 2023

Mee
Chopra

https://youtube.com/shorts/1HhLlnbVmz8

https://youtu.be/ww9iwTLzXgE

Vortex of Hues

Tints and tones threading each other
weaving a vortex of hues
at dawn, decked with a soft blush
at dusk, draped in Vermillion and Gray
I become a tissue of moods.

Am I ensnared within a prism
spinning in a deceptive spectrum?

Darkness and light
embellish diverse tones
countless complexions interlace
basking in the sun's grace.

During my shadowy chase
of the setting sun
twilight seeps into me
retracing the footsteps.

In my joyous laughter
I gleam with golden light
in sorrow, I embody discerning silver
occasionally bronzed
savouring the bitter and sweet alike.

https://youtu.be/Rm5DGZcr8yw

Am I a pallette of
enduring expressions
across the fiery time and space?

Every passing day
a stroke of inspiration
urging my brush to sway
painting an epic beyond—

A Palette of Expressions

https://youtube.com/shorts/4_QI6CMwDjc

Mute Presentiment

Each yearning shadow
an elongated finger
peeling layers
a veiled existence
steps into a *karmic* reversal
within time's labyrinthine cartography
unravelling stories
meeting my alter ego
unlocking a multitude of shattered doors
searching gems behind
treasures that time could not shackle.

I discern the twilight
a fleeting heartbeat
pulsating and palpable
time morphs in my hands
transforming into
my mother's trusted walking stick
guiding me into the life's uncertainties.

A journey through a forgotten trail
tracing the faint footsteps
that I, in a haste, left untraced.

Meena
Chopra

https://youtu.be/7L5JeKGMJXk

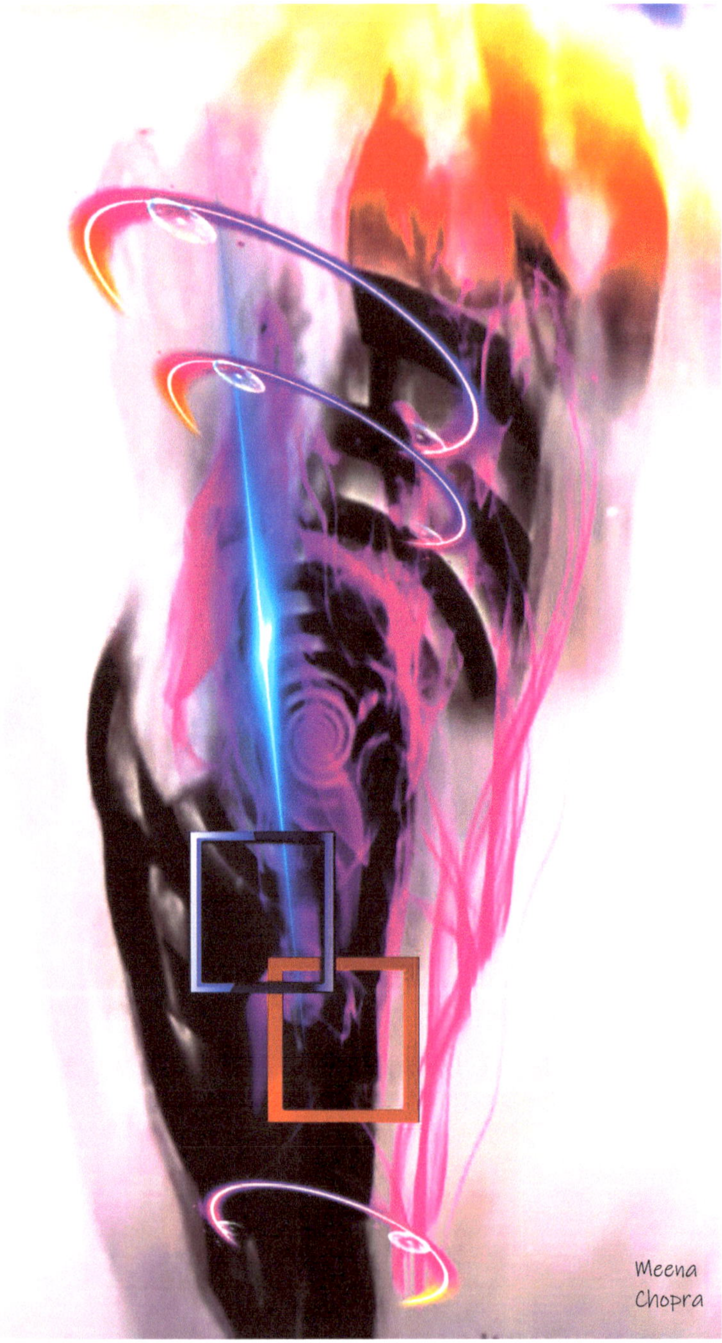

https://www.youtube.com/shorts/1BA3yxlkZgc

Orbital Silence

Life, a spinning carousel
each revolution, a fleeting memory
an augmented past of layered illusions
spiralling, a dance of flexing reflections.

Every turn, a transient feeling
staged on time's shelf
pictures frozen in crystal frames
peep out to stare at me
these gazing echoes multiply
within my eye's orbit.

The stillness replicates
connecting the continuity of past
with its participle
pulsating with the binary heartbeat
chasing the whispers
of distant generations
halting the moments
within universal divergence.

Thoughtful Muse

Thoughts sparkle and sprawl
floating on my laptop screen
whirling, smoothly navigating
within the layers of my gaze
reaching the dragon cage of my heart
unzipping a serpentine crackle
shedding old skin
renewing fossilized attire
pirouetting hidden archives
punctuating certainties.

An insightful inspiration
melts the sprawling icy words
A bubbling potion
mixes and concocts meanings.

Enigmatic vapours rise, tickling the senses
I ingest the sharp flavour
in return, the flavour consumes me
I savored the essence
a lifetime encapsulated in an instant.

The screen blinks into darkness
stilling my under-covered soul.

Deadpanned winter solstice
celebrates the longest dark hours.

Daylight conserved
in the glow of my laptop's display.

Charismatic Chiaroscuro by Meena Chopra

https://youtu.be/bQ8twz_2ROg

https://youtu.be/bJhYVc02Dlo

Saptarishi *

The day unrolled
as I sketched the Moon
with golden ink in the sunlight.

Stars scattered
across the night sky
unfurling the zodiac patterns.

The Great Bear, The Big Dipper,
seven stars, seven sages
with their shining wisdom
echoing through time
collapse in a light-polluted sky.

Constellations sigh
thousands of years trickled
composing and computing
narratives and legends
versifying my days and nights.

The Little Dipper stirred
celestial slumber disturbed
preluding a new journey.

Steadfast and unwavering
the radiant star, *Dhruv**
navigates my way
in the clusters of space
light years sweep by.

*P165

Charismatic Chiaroscuro by Meena Chopra

Meena
Chopra

https://youtu.be/dzOxia1Ctys

The Dewdrop

A small bead of dew
submerged in eternity
dodging the clutches of misty damp nights
caressing and grasping a fleeting leaf
clinging and nestling on the swaying bough.

A brief salvation!

Longing, craving, and dreaming
holding onto aspirations and wishes
preceding its fall
surrenders to earth
becoming dust
returning to soil
transforming to ashes.

Concluding—
The circle of life?

Translated from my Hindi poem

A Handful of Daylight

A withered dawn
tip-toeing
beyond the dark glitter.

A tiny star
riding the light beam
enters through the skylight
touching my skin
twinkling at the sunrise.
.

A warm, amber glow
envelops the room.
Its essence seeping into every pore
of the budding dawn.

My body soaks the soul
the day unfurls
as a butterfly swirls around the lone star
I hear a birdsong
a serenade unfolds
over the sill.

A handful of daylight
spilling stars in the sky
embodies the chirping
infusing life into the morning chorus
each nook illuminated by a tender warmth.

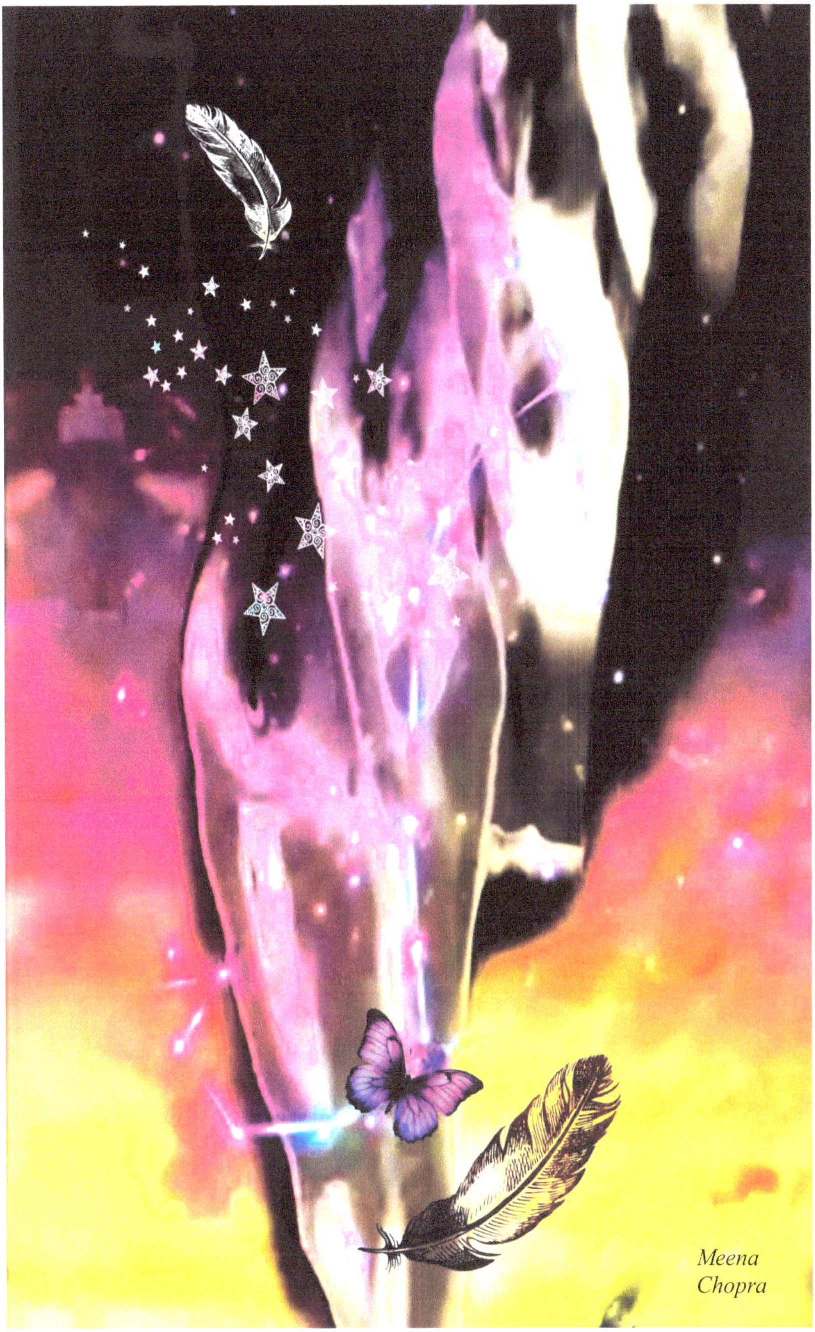

https://youtube.com/shorts/uRRF4ySuC1c

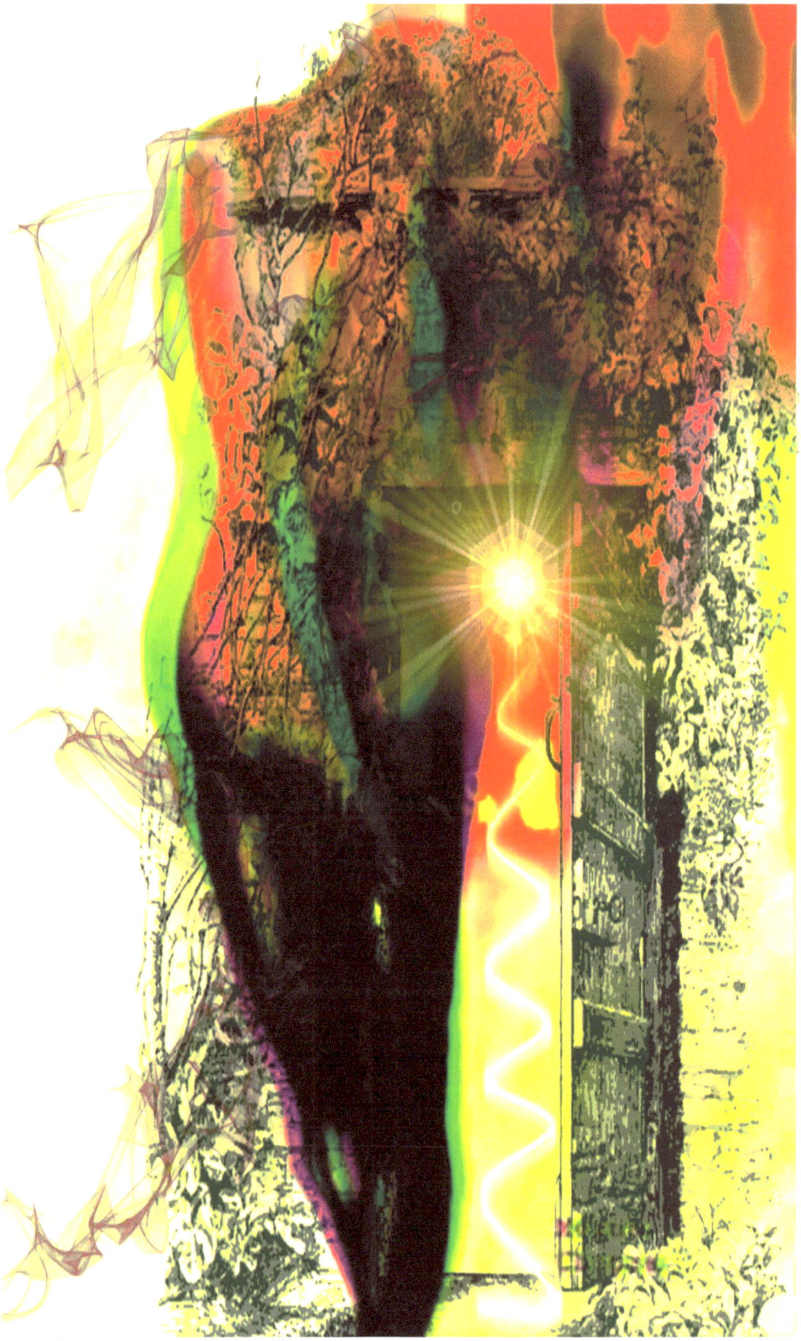

https://youtu.be/JbXjNIbjlXQ

A Dream Sequence

I run, endlessly chasing shadows
through a long narrow corridor
flanked by countless
old, fragile, termite-ridden wooden doors,
surfaces, etched with the scars of time.

I knock, but they do not open.
I pound, but they remain sealed.
Relentlessly, I hit hard
seeking entry to the enigma beyond
turning and twisting the handles in vain
inserting keys from my jumbled bunch
all mixed up
a chilled weariness creeps
through my bones.

I catch a fleeting glow
a frail luminosity
seeping through the fissures in the doors
a desire, I believe
it may thaw my frozen spirit.

Suddenly, at the end of the gallery
a large door, diamond-studded,
swings open before me

I step into a resplendent vista
enraptured and overwhelmed
I wake up
shrouded in a white mist.

A rhapsody lingers on
embracing the nihility.
A reality of my dream sequence.

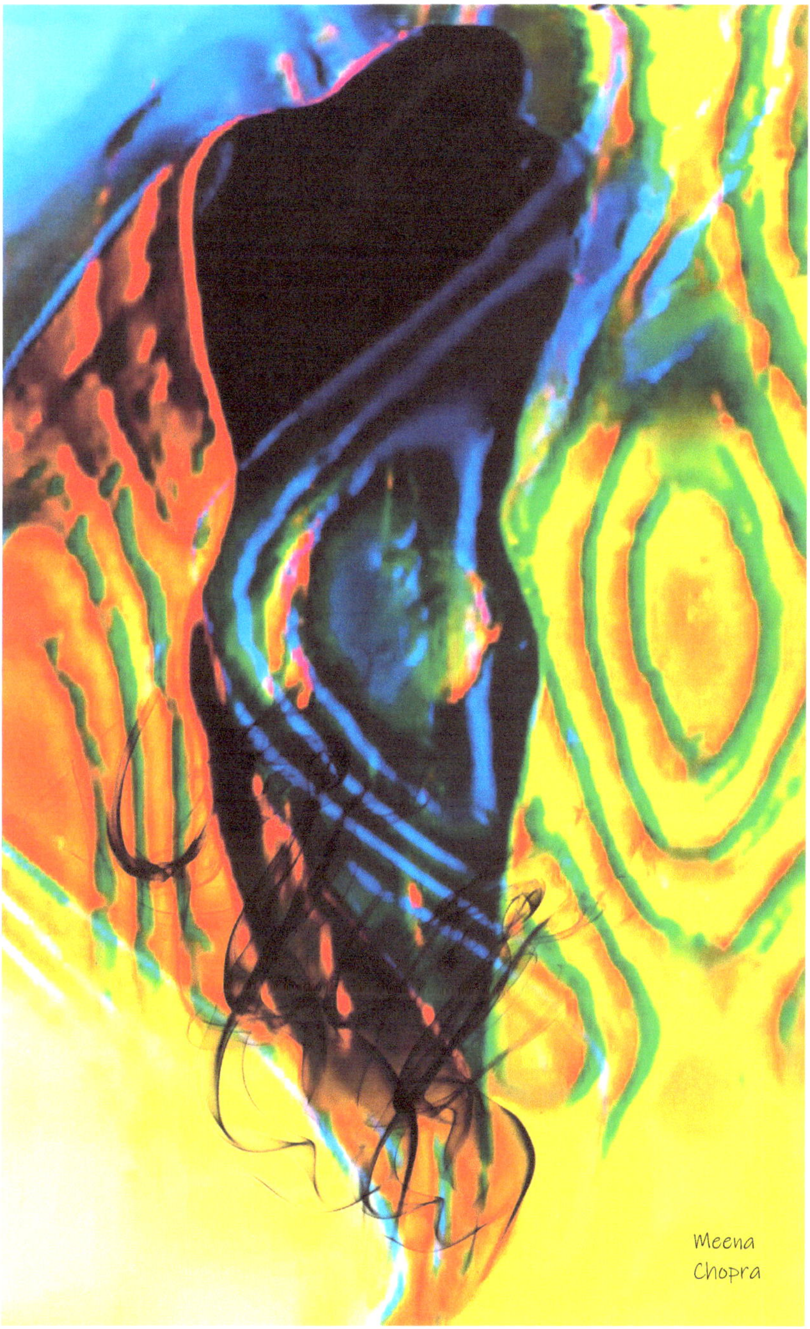

Night, a weary shade of black

https://youtu.be/5P6HCWtneus

https://youtube.com/shorts/smq_T1u6nc4

Lingering Impressions

I enter the light
shedding the night's integument
shadows resurface
Hovering.
A recursive pattern
comes and goes.

Algorithms dissolve and evolve
emerging with sweat
dripping to the earth.

My feet damp
soaked and soiled
yet, I forge ahead
struck by lightning.
A tornado whirls through my body
I remain motionless
tremors cascading
shadows fade.

A swift current trudges along
sensations linger on
stirring aging silhouettes
residing in me
analogous to my body contours.

Charismatic Chiaroscuro by Meena Chopra

Silent glory of 'Port Credit' by Night

Bright neon beam drizzles down
from the lighthouse
shimmering waters on rugged rocks
breaking the silence of silver-patinas.

Ashen moonlight
stars sentinels
soft gentle breeze on my cheeks.

Like the water
I am swamped in silence.

Heavens fall
Sky is empty!

Charismatic Chiaroscuro by Meena Chopra

https://youtu.be/T3K32AmeNDo

https://youtube.com/shorts/wfbrnnve9Ok

Mississauga: A City Becoming

Mississauga at fifty—
a cityscape layered with time's trowel
where rivers once carved silent paths
now streets pulse with unspoken stories.

The land remembers its old roots
even as towers climb skyward,
etching new lines into the horizon.
From the quiet breath of Lake Ontario
to the hum of voices that blend and rise
cultures merge
each trail weaving its mark
on the city's heart.

Change is not gentle here,
but bold, restless, surging forward
carrying with it echoes of what was
and dreams of what will be—
Mississauga, never still
always becoming.

Charismatic Chiaroscuro by Meena Chopra

Corona Kaal

Wintery soil in my hands, wet and cold
mixed with salt and snow
I freeze in the damp deep lines of my palm.

Icy and wet
I see the sun
sitting on my window sill
dark and frozen
embracing the frosty warmth.

The Siberian sky
above me
gray and nippy
peeping from the skylight.

Time swept away in a blink
this was an immersive year
The *'Corona Kaal.'**

Halting, reflecting
and measuring
calculating and computing
I loved this osmosis for a change
A necessary evil of my passing years.

https://youtu.be/dhtKUrXqjk8

*P167

Osmosis

https://youtu.be/LDFiPp8WSeo

Whimsical

A maze tunnels inside me
my favourite hiding spot
where I often underpass
sunken and trembling
ruminating and reflecting.

A deep-set blank stare
follows me everywhere
a vacuumed cornet hollows my ears
cracking the labyrinth
Stone-deaf!

A forest grows in and out of me
chasing me to the cliff edge
beyond which
an abyssal darkness
engulfs the red-rimmed sun.

Numerous shadows melt
forming a phantasmagorical backdrop
in the sky-ocean
swamped to rise again.
My vision spins
caught up in the life's wheel.

Perhaps, freedom is just a notion
a whim of some poet or a madman?

Charismatic Chiaroscuro by Meena Chopra

Meena
Chopra

 https://youtu.be/drfyjo9XIPk

A Silent Cocoon
(during the pandemic)

Life, a turbulent stage with visions fogged
a whirlwind of uncharted destinies
entrapped in a ceaseless run
drifting clouds smudge the vivid landscapes
a spectral mist obfuscates the defining outlines
our shared laughter and sorrows
veiling the future in a shrouded uncertainty.

Dreams evaporate
leaving behind the ache of lost sounds
where silenced voices echoed
through the caverns of isolation
overwhelmed and insulated.
Hands tremble groping for a healing solution.

The brilliance of solitude
seemingly eclipsed
starkly stared at me
penetrating my muffled spirit
cocooned in a yearning time.

The order in chaos
an uncanny offering of the pandemic
met the challenges of the regressing humanity
transforming and reflecting
the hollow human corridors
a labyrinthine mortality
entire journey eternally vivified.

Charismatic Chiaroscuro by Meena Chopra

Co-travelling with a Quill

My quill
brimming with your radiance
inked memories spill a midnight rain
sprinkling words on paper.
A dream river ripples
flowing through pages
illuminating a new life story.

Such mastery in this pen
blending with my fingertips
traversing with you
treading softly together
a simmering journey
rising through flames
beyond the setting sun.

Charismatic Chiaroscuro by Meena Chopra

Translated from Hindi

Meena
Chopra

A Pulsing Umbra

Ashen mornings, graying evenings
endings and beginnings
in a perpetual motion
defined to a determined orbit.

As evening falls, cascading lustres
a silver sombre of a drizzling night canvas
pouring on my heartbeats
soft currents spurting out
various shapes and lines falling into each other
collapsing within, streaming forth
illuminating an agile fantasy
shadows frescoed on my soul.

Life courses through my veins
subtle images float in my watery vision
each one a vaporous film
moving in the boundless universe
of my retinal fluid.

I treasure every closure
I revel in every origin
I find solace in every ripple.

Charismatic Chiaroscuro by Meena Chopra

https://youtube.com/shorts/RsDk5gk3H_8

Meena
Chopra

https://youtu.be/FGEkKLJMXBE

95

A brief metamorphosis unfolds
amidst the interlacing shadows
a retreat in time.

Roots stretch from sky to ground
raw yet tender
pivoting with riveting precision
the pendulum of destiny
retracing steps in a lunar penumbra
etching a resolute path
towards a pulsing umbra.

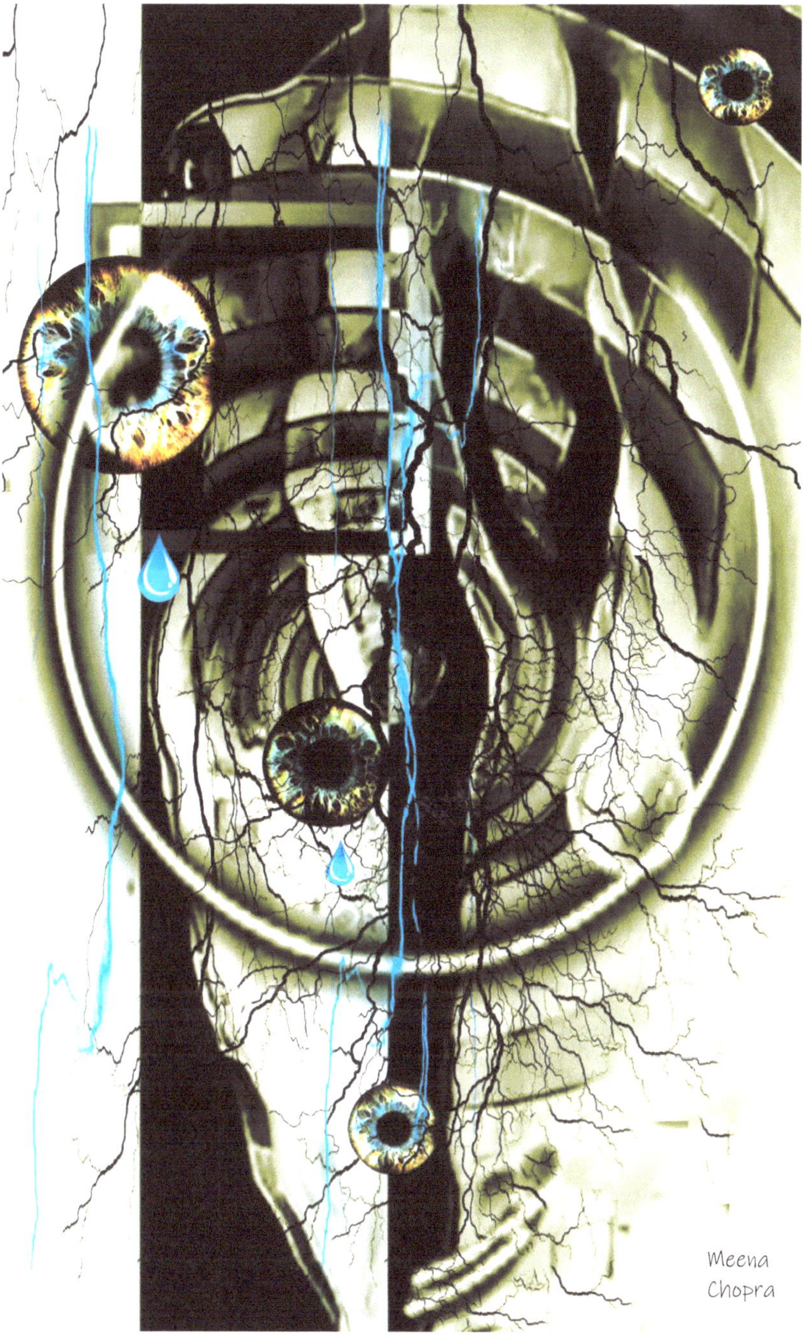

Pendulum

Meena
Chopra

https://youtu.be/xqp9LtyMa4g

Lotus-Sky

I woke up, floating on a fluffy cotton cloud
cocooned in a velvety cosmos
where asteroids stitched my dream sequence
humming waves of the Milky Way
strumming my ears.

A white foam curls around me
lacing me in an ethereal elegance
a nonstop rhythm enters my skin
an iridescent riverlet passes
through a sparkling night
carrying my luminescent vision
to distant galaxies.

Tender tendrils of stardust
caressing my face
etching constellations on my cheeks.

A lotus-sky, lures my eyes
perfumed petals falling all over me
a fragile fragrance lingered
weaving serenity from my skin to the sky.

I saw *Vishnu** emerging
draped in the mysteries of a yellow sunset
holding a lilac-pink lotus in his one palm
a resonating conch shell, a spinning *chakra*
and a tough mace in the other three.

*P165

98

Meena
Chopra

Resting in a meditative mood
reclining and floating on *Shesh-Shaiyya**
his 'couch of the coiled snake.'

In his deep trance, *Vishnu* counts *kalpas**
through the stills and spins of his *chakra.*
eonic waves glide underneath
a timeless current sustains the infinity.

Majestic serpent hoods
crowned with the radiance of a million suns
shelter galaxies and planets in resplendence
the serpentine grace guarding them.

Amidst turbulent and frothy sea waters
Adishesh*, the ancient protector
descends to the nether world
winding the threads of time
solidifying the earth
nurturing its core
sustaining humanity.

The eternity carries the earth on its shoulders
stabilizing the tremors of time
Adishesh becomes the celestial anchor.

Life ticks forward
while *Vishnu** ruminates

*P165   *P167

Charismatic Chiaroscuro by Meena Chopra

Meena
Chopra

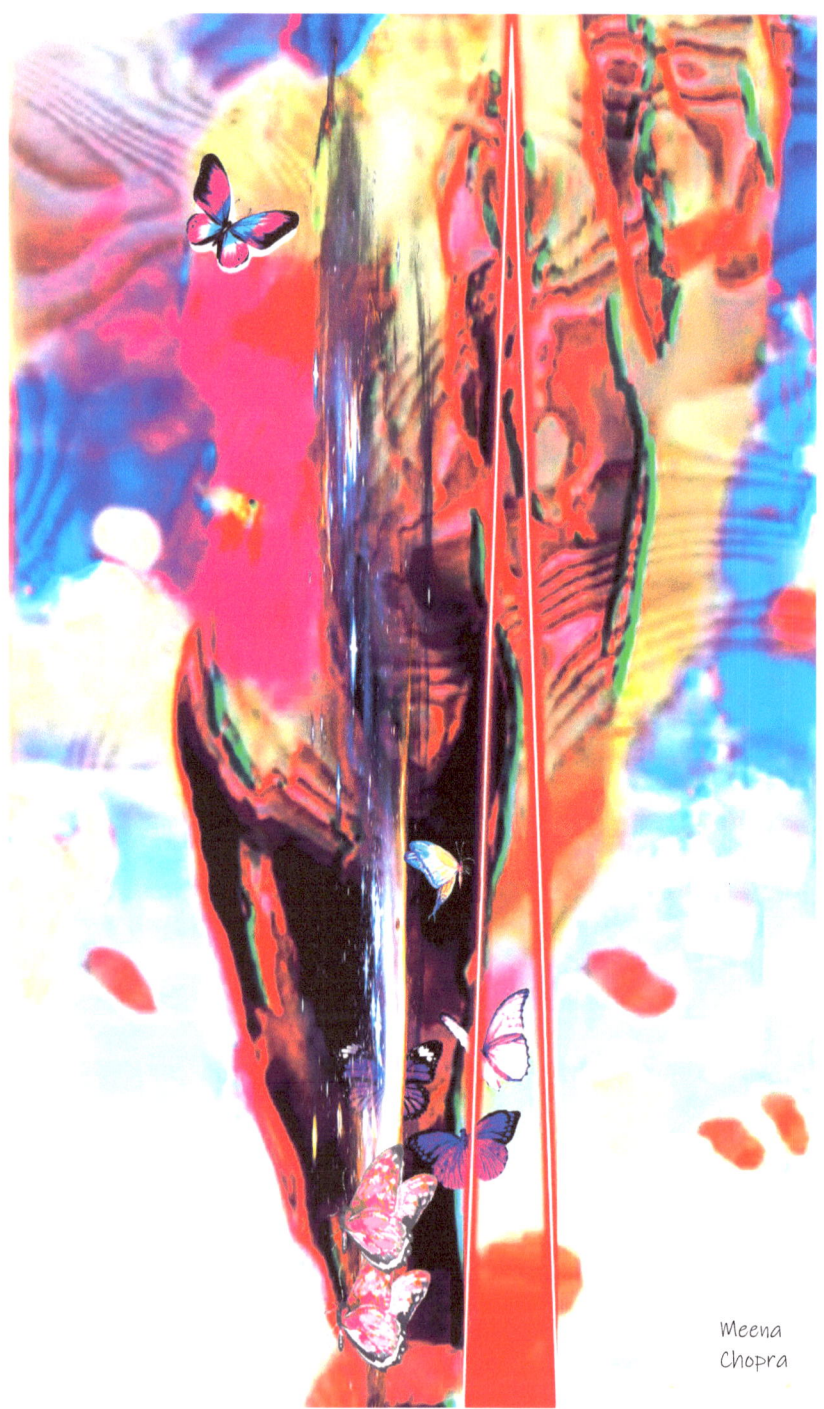

Meena
Chopra

musing on his *Anant-Shaiyya**
delving into the mysteries of existence.
contemplating a new venture
blooming into another dawn.

Butterflies soar on my lilac-ash skin
lotus unfurls in a scarlet-blue sky
petals, soaking in the ripples of my eyes.

Meena
Chopra

Liquid Moments

As I stroll
time ripples under my feet
a river dark and flowing
liquid moments
snuggled in the water's bosom
wet soil holds secrets
a long-lost past
roots dig deep.

Life continues to roll
I tread the fluidity
my feet afloat
my heart buoyed up.

Currents stream deep below
a writhing flow rises
slowly wrinkling in an upsurge
I slide away in a passing breeze.

Thus years glide by—

Charismatic Chiaroscuro by Meena Chopra

Me - And My Himalayan Soul

A camouflaged dreamer
draped in rustic ethnicity
craving for crisp fresh air.

I, a Himalayan spirit in a jungle city
a small-towner forever traversing
through narrow lanes and verdant paths
chasing a dimming horizon
beyond the concrete wilderness
yellow gold of a rusty sun pigmented me.

Night, a weary shade of black
choked with lazy stars
fading into the silent fray
a gentle breeze

A remote standoffish gaze, stagnant
dominoes masquerade
their silken threads clinging to my skin.

The vibrant city, Toronto
drenched in a fervour, tap dancing.
Night's cadence
grooving my ear-holes
amidst the wilting petals and leaves
a reverberating saffron

Meena
Chopra

Meena
Chopra

lilted the scaling clouds
above the towering skyscrapers
rushing autumn odour
fiery orange and red
sprinkled all over
initiating a modern mantra
in-between
Me - and My Himalayan soul.

Streetscape

Walking the streets in Toronto
filled with cigarette smoke
acrid fumes trespassing
my nostrils and lungs
encroaching my breath
trapped under the alleys
of giant skyscrapers.

City exhales toxic whispers
stifling the air
making my throat parched
caught up in a frequent sip of a diet Pepsi.

Eyes socialize on the cell phone-screen
occasionally lookup
craving for a spotless sky
groping the traces
the rare fresh air
ready to clinch
an evasive breeze
caught up in the modern muddle of tech taste
alluring an up and coming generation.

I adjust my eyeballs, squinting
as cornea melts
blurring my vision
in the shadows of bustling Union Station

https://youtube.com/shorts/PkFi4aDGG3k

I see a woman
pregnant and homeless
begging for her livelihood
pleading mercy for the soul within.

Humanity cries—
the stark inequalities of our urban landscape
hover the skyline
while they claim—
'We are rich, prosperous and progressing'.

At this moment,
amidst the ticking numbers
on the linear clock
my trembling fingers fumble
for the snippets of inspiration
while inhaling city surroundings
inspirited, to inscribe human lullabies
on the heaving pages
of my trapped breath
holding a fume-filled pen in my hand.

https://youtube.com/shorts/KTnyEFktPdE

Potter's Twilight

The evening falls
A malleable gold-gray darkness
descends in my palms.

Soft clay like
moving in my supple fingers
ready to be shaped
carved, and moulded
to be fired in the radiant sun
turning into a glowing earthenware
whirling in terracotta dreams.

This *diva** of light
was enshrined on the evening's doorsill
The dusk illuminated a coming night.

Shadows underneath the glowing flame
flickered with a twilight
exuberating potter's delight.

*P166

Sailing Through the Mediterranean

Sea waves whisper ancient secrets
the sun spills its golden ink
on the Mediterranean
reflecting a dance of silver and gold.

Daylight fades
vivid waters reflect in my eyes
a far off ship in twilight's grasp, vanishes
silhouettes shimmer.

Gone— Lost in a blink.

Droplets of stars
fragile as dreams
soothe my aching eyes.

I look up
as they trickle through my grasp
slithering away
like the grains of night's sand
carrying a silence
shrouded in mysteries of ancient shores
a few placid moments
of my fleeting journey
their elusive currents
ripple in the vast ocean
silky threads
slipping through my fingers.

Mediterranean breeze
cool on my cheeks
worships eternity.
Sunlight pierces the deep-sea

Grains of Night Sand

Meena Chopra

dusky vignettes melt
descending from the skyline
finding solace in the silent seabed.

Countless tales devoured by the waves
generations lost
entombed underwater
shipwrecks enmeshed in coral reefs
slowly freeing.

Silver streaks rise to the surface
riding the crest of high tides
in a star-studded sky, on a moonlit night.

The day breaks
sun rises on the ocean.

Damp shadows of the past
evaporate as noon arrives
invisible now, lost in the sky.

https://youtu.be/rS875BpiDxo

120

Seven Colours

The nebulous fleeting softness
rising from a dripping rainbow.

Falling drops
wet on the window-sill
reflecting in my sultry eyes
I saw the sky in its stillness
sinking in a frenzy.

A broad daylight
watching me in my true subdivision
fuzzy and hazy
whirl-pooling
deflecting
dispersing a spectrum.

Because
once upon a time
I got steeped
in seven colours.

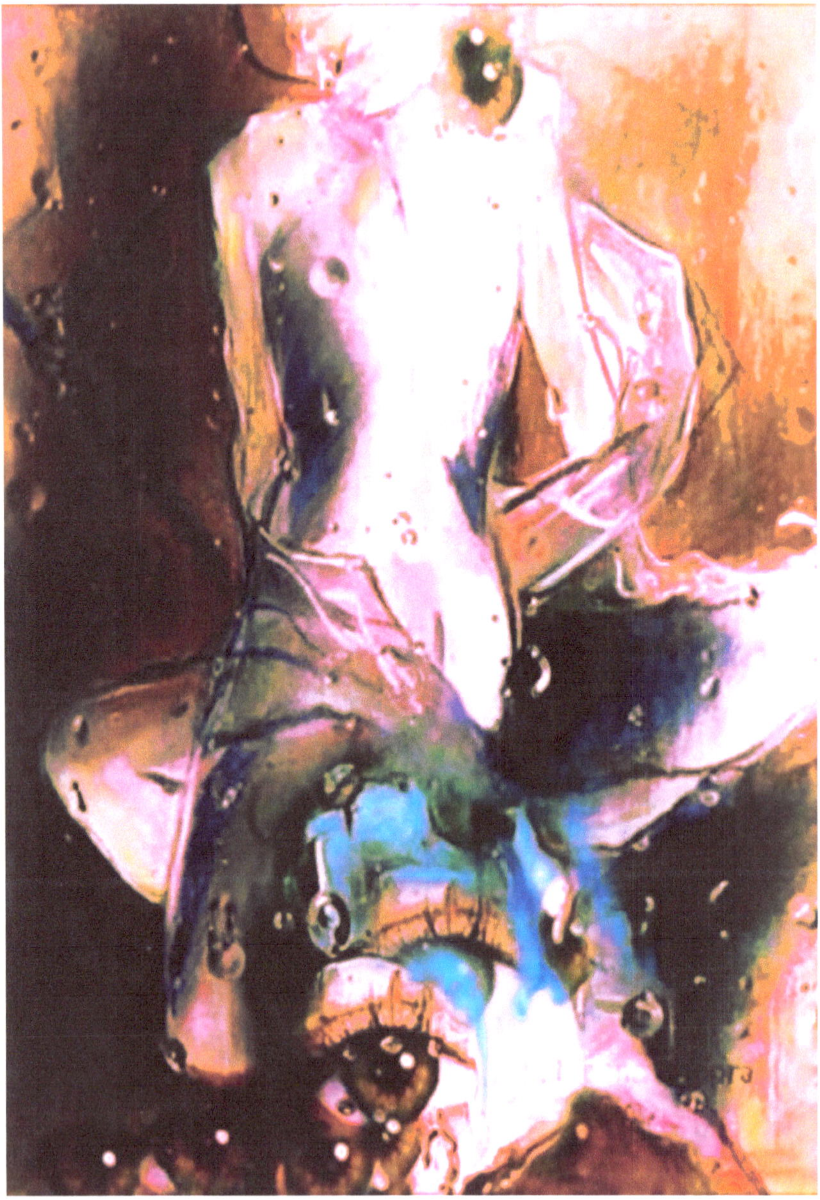

https://youtu.be/FSyicDHRpuk

Seasonal Scroll

The ages scroll down
unrolling a backdrop
seasons change in a smooth flow.

Spring's tender blooms flowering into summer
vitalizing vivid colours
reaching the sky
sunflowers bathed, their faces aglow.

A quiet rustle seizes the brilliance of autumn
ablaze in fiery reds and gold
leaves flutter, fall under my feet
hues dissolve in my eyes
moistening me, sweeping my heart
leaving its marks on my core.

Fall air clings to my breath
it's fragrance deep in my soul
immersed in the sepia of an old Polaroid
each frame, a snapshot
a precious remembrance.

Each blink crystallizes a moment
a hazy essence lingers on my lashes
raindrops dewed every memory
petrichor droplets all over my skin
I am drenched in a vintage scent.

A hint of a mist passes over
a slight shiver nips my gaze
my body tremors.

Winter is on its way
with snow-white celebrations
a silvery sombte freezes me
frosty days are ahead.

https://youtu.be/H_2mE_7yKVY

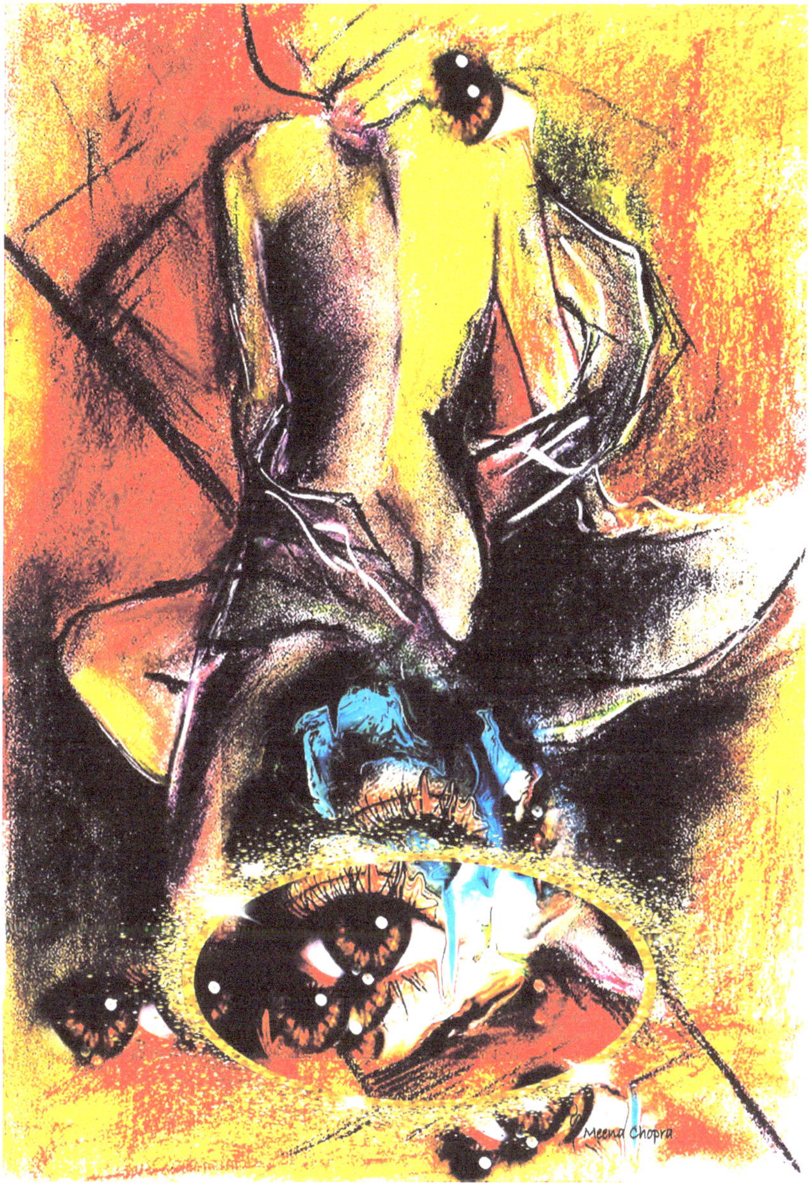

https://www.youtube.com/shorts/4ZxT1JZ5WIk?feature=share

Meena
Chopra

https://youtu.be/uTz_65Oypq8

Colours of Ages

Flavours of ancestral stories
gently seep, seasoning me
with many shades.

Tableaux spice my senses
snippets sketched on antiquity
saturate me in a mythical era.

Fixed and meditative
my eyes discern
moods and tonalities
orchestrating the melodies.

A gentle rustle
of a colorful linen sways.
My mother's *saree**
clinging to my damp skin
shaping my body waves.
Swinging images linger
wrapping the delicate contours
glowing in multi colours
dancing filaments swell.

A diatonic cocktail of visual sensations
gushes out of me.

Steeped in the hymn of a far-off star
I dissolve into the muslin strains
a receding swish in my ears
echoing through ages.

*P167

A fleeting night tenderly touches me
soothing hues of blue and gray
caress the aching shadows .

Faded colours of an aging linen
follows me everywhere.

Meena
Chopra

Meena
Chopra

Bursting Bubbles

A tranquil within
ignites a burst of bubbles
effusing from my body.

Each bubble
a shimmering star
a jubilant nightingale
soaring solo
drifting in silence.
.

A vivid spectrum expands,
monochromatic to chromatic
widening a vibrant bandwidth.

Clashing wavelengths
passions and serenity
echo within a tunnel of legends
a script of fragmented tales
bridges the gaps in space and time.

Bubbles fade
spheres retreat, orbs disguise slowly
in a reversal flow
fleeting moments
memories echoing all over me.

https://youtu.be/ALBOaG2-d8o

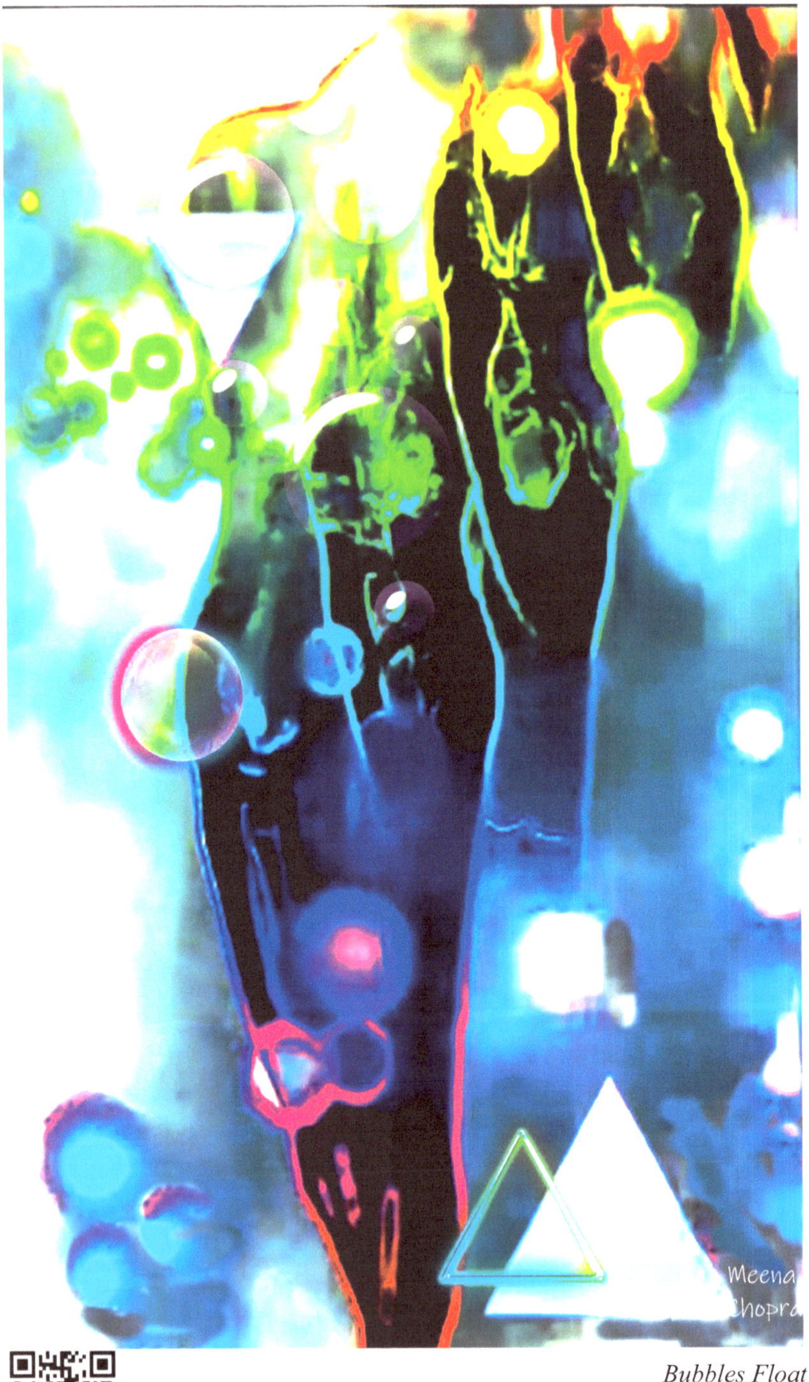

Bubbles Float

https://youtube.com/shorts/lSD4ERQ1aQo

Bubbles Fade

https://youtu.be/VDzVFGpOW6M

Silicon Soul

My eyes tinted with moon-shadow
the sun rises in the east
glittering through my window
golden tendrils softly graze my lashes.

Face radiant with a luster.
dawn pours a liquid gold
hearts melt.

A warmth swirls my blood
my breath expands
a silicon soul circulates in my veins
shaping the rhythm of my days.

My vision shrivels
the sun dips into the cyberspace
dusk unfolds on the window screen.

Night falls, churning algorithms
sky loops in the moonlight
fading shadows float
within the computing clouds.

https://youtu.be/T06D3roj2Oo

Meena
Chopra

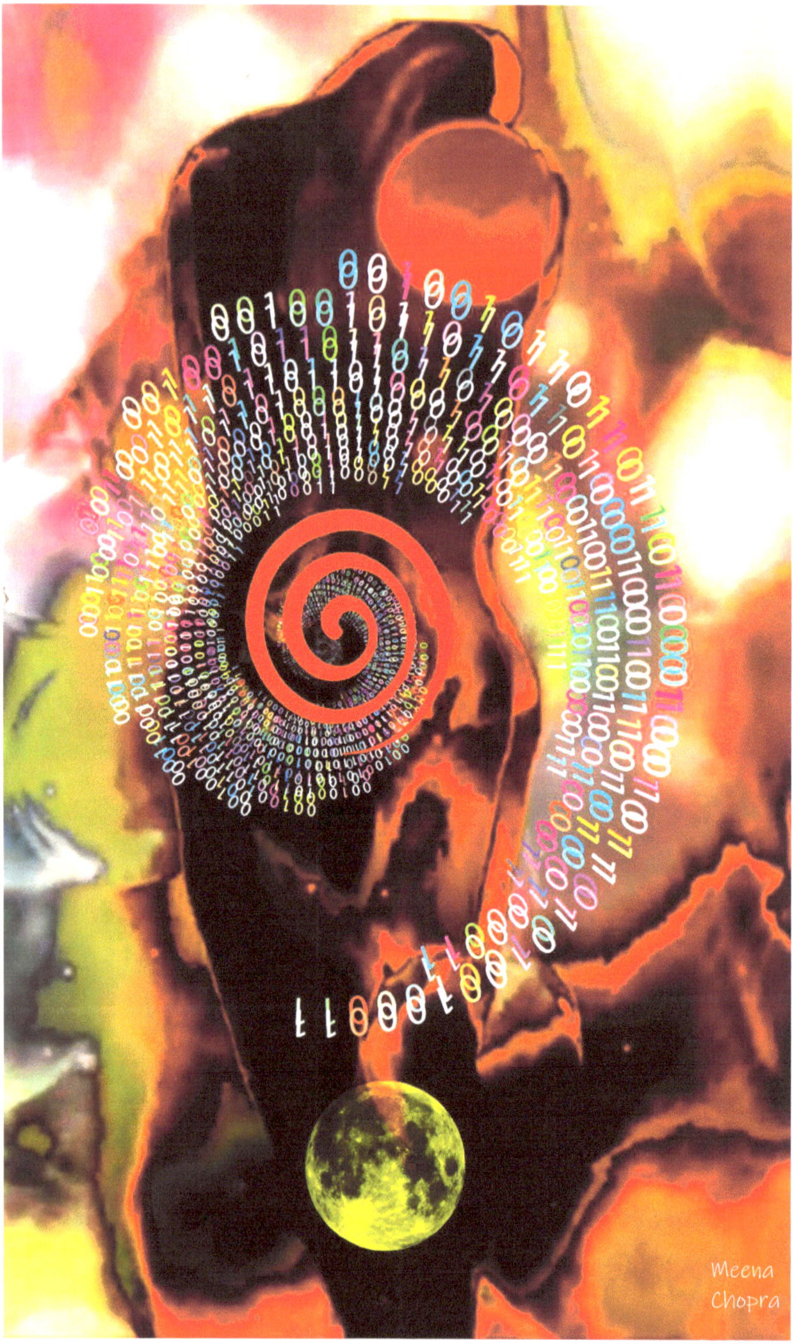

Churning Algorithms

https://youtu.be/BQxscL6hDlc

Digits beat in my heart
my body dehydrates.

I become a nocturnal sprite
a native of a dream space
soaring in a lunar land
leaving no data to be processed.
No black dust, no traces behind
No shadows of networks to find.

https://youtube.com/shorts/MrvkZXPhT60

Meena
Chopra

138

Digital Quandaries

Memories and dreams
intersecting quadrangles and circles
digitized and layered
flowing through
my very being,
converging into a point
pulsing with life's essence
encompassed within squared spaces
unraveling complexities.

Wandering through constrained breaths
capturing frozen moments in life's lens
rushing images, dots, and dashes
interlocked in a patterns
deciphering equations.

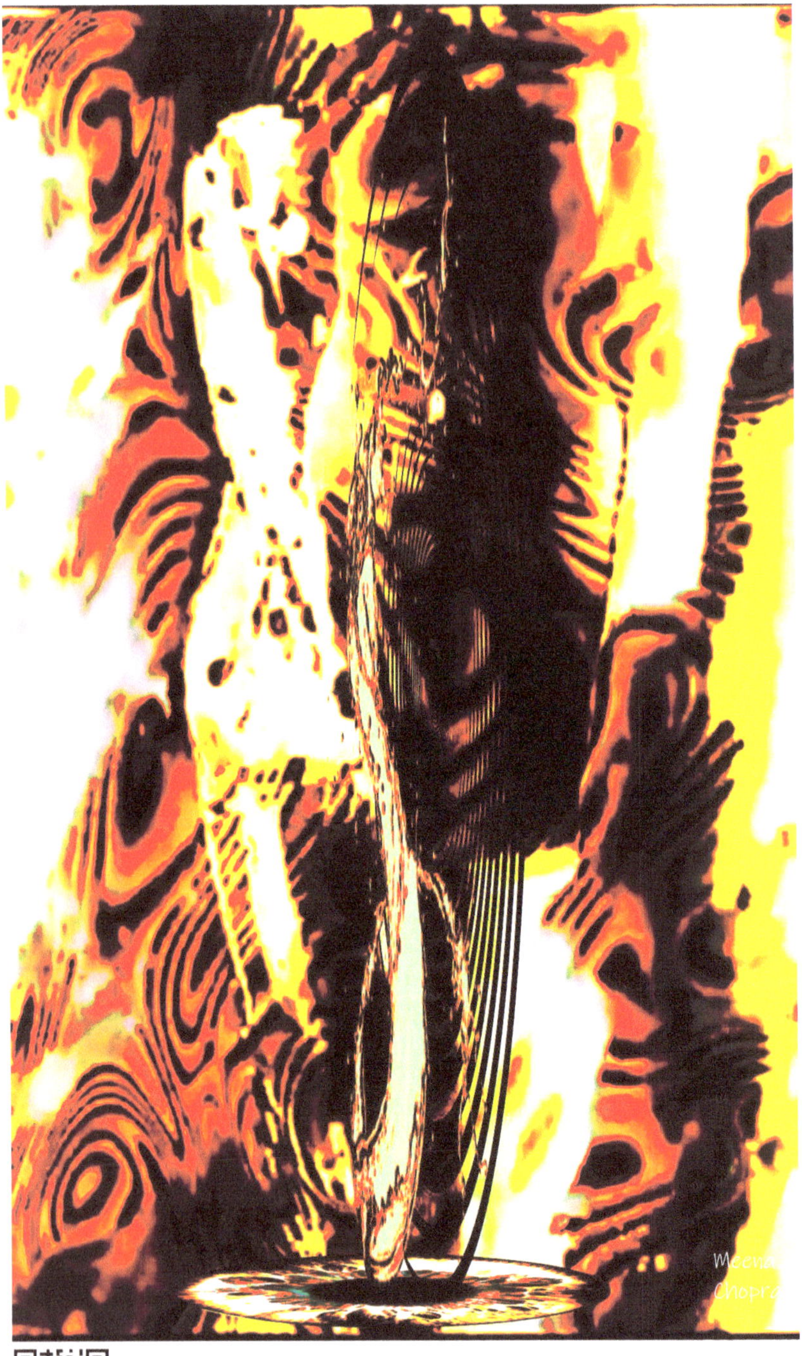

https://youtu.be/HlqG-4CskYA

River Styx flows on—

The night's serpentine creek
rimming on a dark stream
snuggling through my veins
tasting contrasting sensations
a nocturnal feast
The *Stygian* River* flows on—

Desires surge
crashing upon my countenance
I pacify them
calming their storm
immersing in the fluid stare
shadows nestle in my gaze.

An invisible glimpse
wiggles through the water tunnels
finding an escape
from sneaky hideaways
dragging me to my topsoil.

Each sinew
sweats in unison
breathing in the crisp air
renewing an earthly domain.

https://youtube.com/shorts/pI8ESOecSWA

Charismatic Chiaroscuro by Meena Chopra

Shadows, my resolute friends
vanish and return
never abandoning me.

The *Styx River** shivers
persisting in its course
shudders
Flows on—

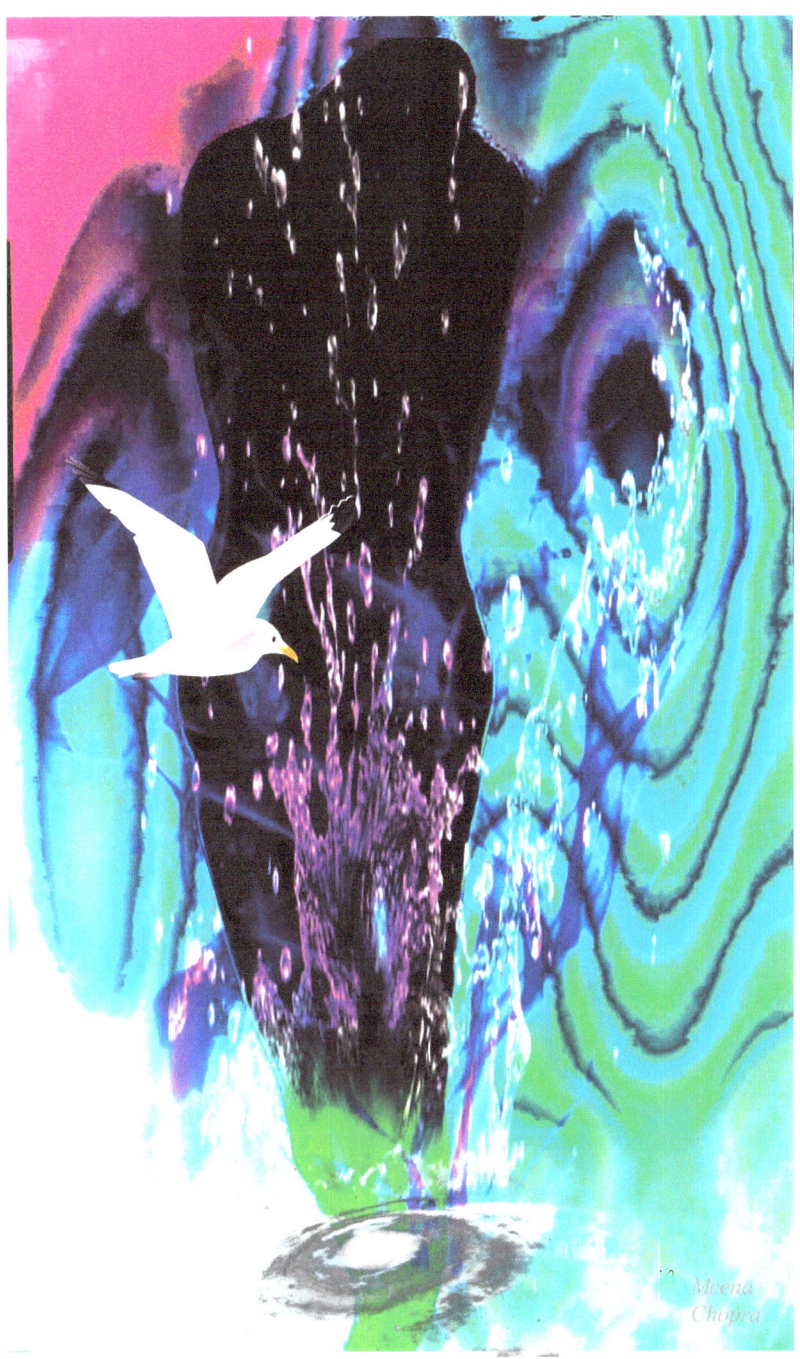

Flows on

Handful of Eternity

I pause, gasp
catch a breath
a deep-sleep mode as
the slumber breaks.

Seven colours flow
tinting the dream cycles
hidden in my dark womb.

Kiss me with a mouthful of eternity
raid me, shred the vizard apart
mould me with clayful reality
seed me with coarse fertility.

An ageless fecundity
a handful agility.

https://youtu.be/VASFp_1pIDQ

145

An Origami of Time and Space

(Inspired by the movie Blade Runner I, and II)

Neons stuttering
Night locked in the metallic grip
reeling through the labyrinth of ambiguous streets
tripping on pavements with fate's hidden cracks.
A cityscape pulsates with nocturnal fervor.

The nearby ocean pulls me
I ride the crest of a colossal wave
a surfer in the night's ocean.
A maelstrom's claws
ensnare me in a chaotic spin.

Foams swirling away from my shoulders
sweeping fragmented replicants
clutching to the sinking saviours.

These cyberpunks emerge
plunging into the swirling turbulence
islanding the surcharged divinities.

Between echoes of self and I—
Is there a blade runner
who may retire these punks?

Between the dots and the lines—
Are there no interludes—a pause
in the script of existence?

Between the vast sky and the boundless sea—
Is there no mystical skyline?

Meena
Chopra

https://youtu.be/UBQZP9ThW88

147

Between the sound and the music—
Are there no lyrical notes
harmonizing the symphonic existence?

Between the moon's silver glow
and the sun's golden warmth—
Do constellations not etch destinies
on the pivoted time?

Between the dimming dusk
and the rising dawn—
Do twilight zones not cast
their elusive shadows?

Between the stages of life and death
within the traces of smoke and dust—
Is there no human yearning?

Between every cause and its effect—
Does karma not simmer, weaving threads
of an eternal destiny?

Between sanctum and sanctorum—
Is there no suspended uncertainty?

Between the dichotomy of anima and animus—
Is there no *Ardhanarishvara**
manifesting paradoxity of dual existence?

*P166

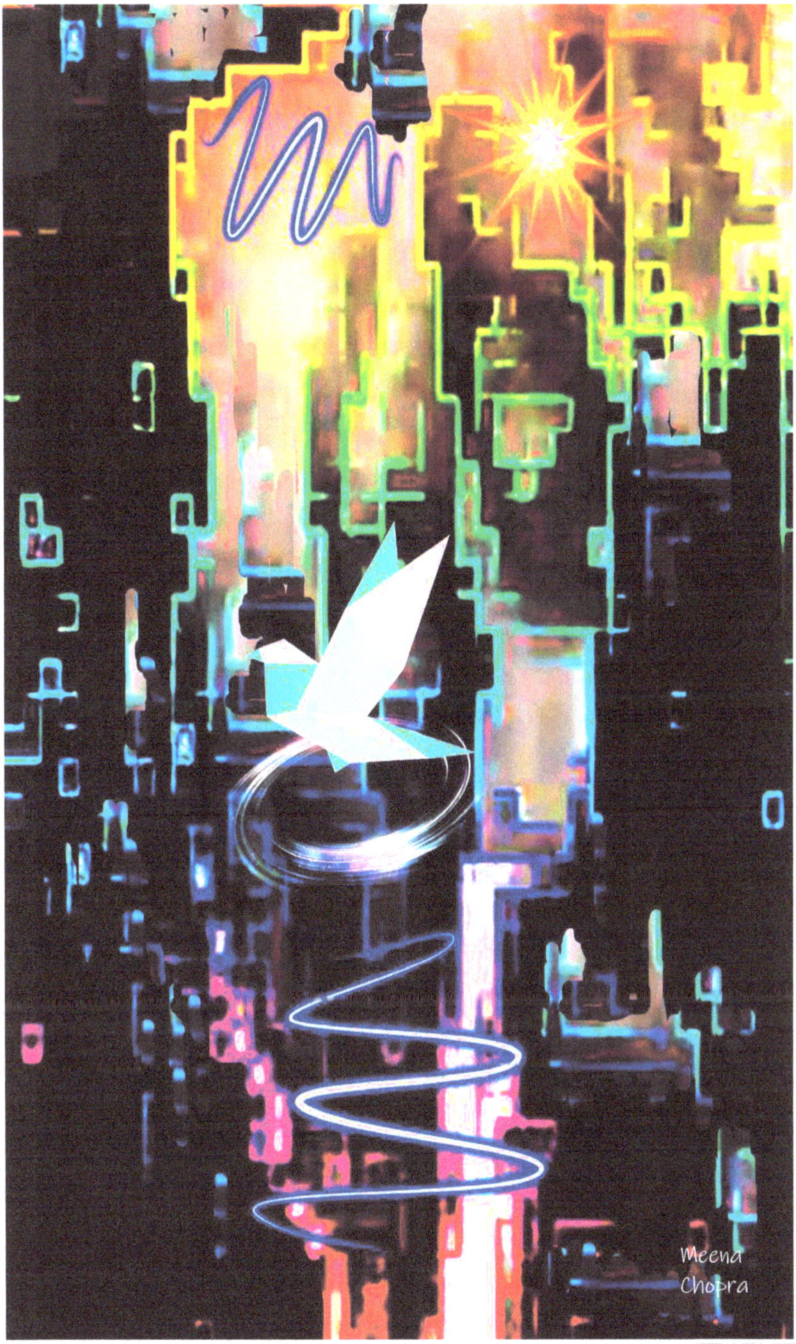

https://youtu.be/p6ichLU1ONk

Between alluring Venus and swift Mercury—
Is there no homogeneous hermaphrodite
transcending gendered boundaries?

And
Between the blade and the blade runner—
Is there no personified emancipator
liberating souls from their own shells?

Or
Is it an iridescent eye!
A gaze, piercing through the illusions of existence.?
Searing through decay and age
a scene-shifter treads
the fine line of a perilous razor's edge?

Or, an origami of time and space
on the doorsteps of a hallucinating nihility?

Or, is it an excavated future
Tunneled in time?

https://youtu.be/UVt2ncvjK_c

Smeared Ash Streaks

I seek myself
amidst the untamed woods
where weed seedlings burgeon into saplings
evolving in deep meditative forests.

Sometimes, I seek my essence
in the sharp crescent of the moon curve
softly shining in the velvet night sky
embossing my orbital vision.

I search for myself
in the mysteries of smeared bone-ash
enigmatic streaks on *Shiva's** forehead.

I search for my vitality
in the might of the tamed time serpent
spiraled around *Shambhu's* neck
amid the interludes of his stilled vision.

In my search for myself
I become a waning leaf
spinning, drifting with the shifting scenes
falling on the earthy Sienna
flurrying in dust
reaching the waves of *Ganga**
rippling down
from the matted braids of *Trishambhu**
flowing through the jungles
yearning to sway on the blue sea tides
cresting the rising rhythm
wandering coast to coast

*P166

Meena
Chopra

https://youtu.be/Rm5DGZcr8yw

153

Meena
Chopra

A half-moon plunges
on the horizons of my eyes.

As I uncover mysteries
a seething quest mists me
shrouding the curved shadows.

The visibility evaporates
silhouettes glow, ethereal embers on my face
their ashen remains
trickle down on my cheeks
shattering the smoky echoes.

Eroding times sift through me—

My residual experiences, tangible now
faces, places, and moments
slowly immerse in the flowing *River Ganges.* *

Re-animated life

Fragments of light
interlace sodden dreams.

Scrape of the full moon
rides the high tide
cresting with waves that
disappear and reappear
settle and rise
along the pulsing shore.
They shine on wet sand.

Shaken by the dreams
I wake up too close to my reality.

Forsaken and fossilized
with passing time
silver-studded wings
shiver and gasp
along the sprawling coastline
malleable now, ready to soar

Lost Password

I sit near a flowing stream
in the cool shade of trees
with my Kindle reader in my hand.

Crystal-clear water
smooth on pebbly stones
sends shivers up my spine
with its refreshing touch.

A soft melody of flowing water
brushes my skin.
Its gentle currents
lead to a lagoon below in a deep valley.

I try to read my book
but my reader refuses to open.
The elusive password slips through my hands
lost in the descending mountain shadows
fingers desperately fumbling to find it.

My lost password eludes me
like a wisp of smoke.
My eyes searched everywhere
couldn't help but wonder
if it held the key to a story yet to unfold.

My reader stays closed.

Tired eyes see a shadow-play
as the darkness falls

I can faintly hear the echo of the fading brook.
A gentle breeze rustles through the hidden pages
stirring the words to leap out
cascading ink seeking the light.

Shadows recede in the valley below.
scattered in the meadow
words transmute into fireflies
acquiring dainty wings that coil
soaring across the river
diving into the dark lagoon
penetrating the core
where my password is ensnared
in a mesmerizing whirlpool.

Words pull the drenched password
out of the strong whirling water currents
they spiral into many ancient tales
sodden in time, obscured from eyes.

The sun goes down
beyond the mountain stream
shedding a warm glow.
My Kindle opens
pages of my book shine
enriched with the essence of extinct lores.

Words gleam, stories unfold
A twilight shimmers in my eyes.

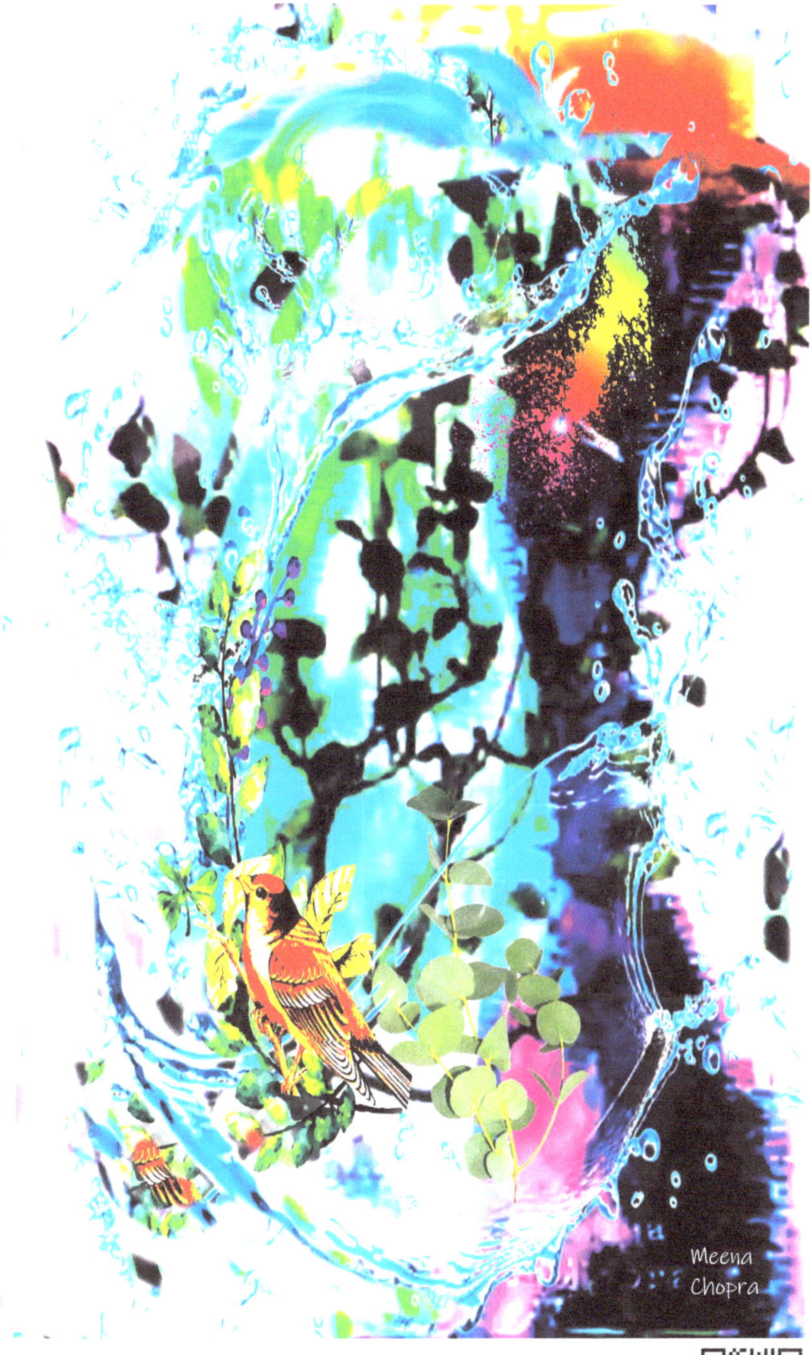

https://youtube.com/shorts/DpcxA7Dk024

https://youtu.be/-YZZ8aX2ZTo

Under the Pilkhan Tree

We met and sat
musing with books in our hands
turning each page
unveiling verses, fables and tales
with each falling leaf
Under the *Pilkhan tree**.

As the time passed
words revolved, condensed and spiraled
climbing high, reaching the dense crown
to be cured and dried in sun
imbibed and nurtured in the sap
preserved in the wood of the knobby trunk
protected by the bark
silver-washed for ages to come.

Branches grew, sprouting into tiny buds
resonating in generations
time swirled, legacies unfurled
stories sighed.
A light breeze
beneath the bearded tree.

*Dedicated to all the fellow writers who gather under the
generosity and warmth of Pilkhan Tree for readings, at
Prof.Malashri and Robey's residence in New Delhi*

*P166

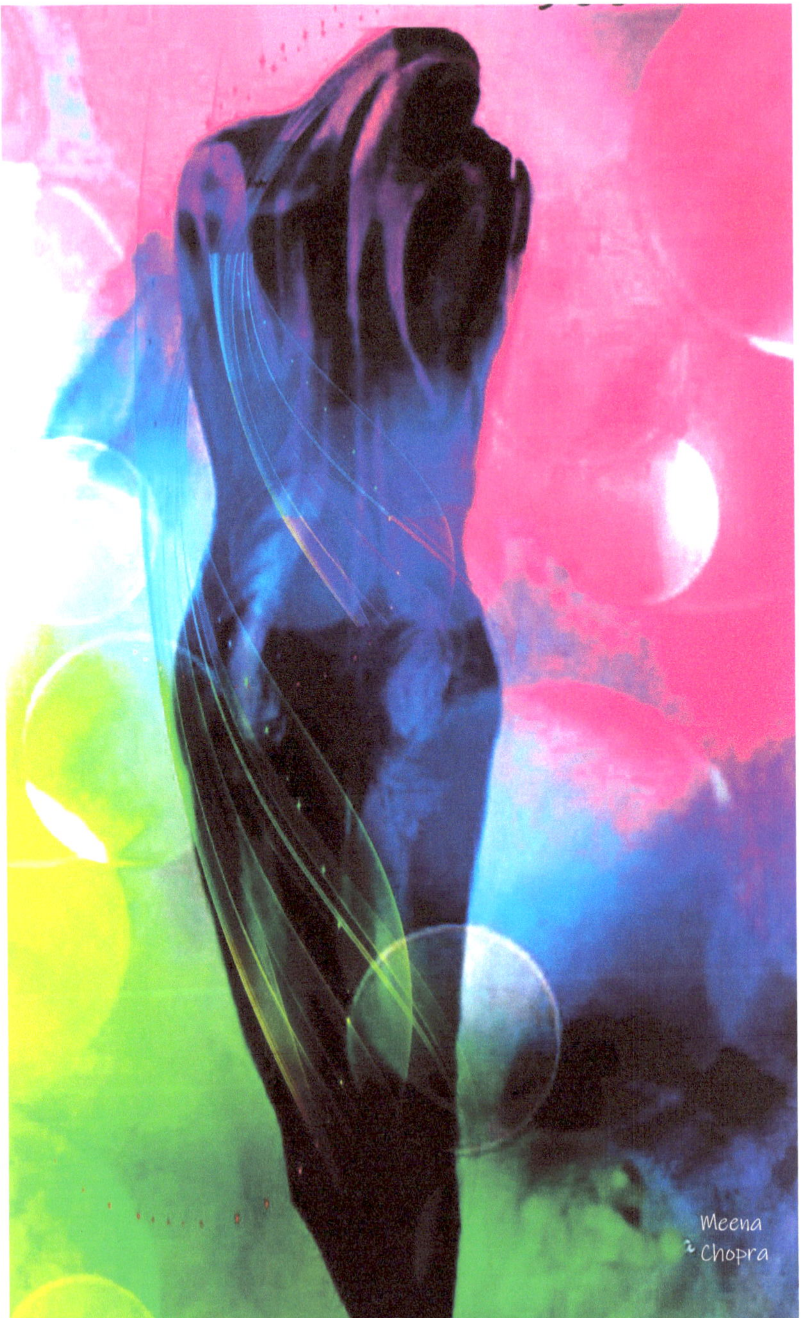

https://youtu.be/mUi-Kz6BN7o

Appendix

Brahma, Vishnu Mahesh*P39: Three forms or trinity is the trinity of supreme divinity in Hinduism, in which the cosmic functions of creation, of preservation and destruction are personified as a triad of deities. Typically, the designations are that of *Brahma* the creator, *Vishnu* the preserver, and *Shiva/Mahesh* the destroyer. --Wikipedia

Saptarishis*P71: In ancient Indian astronomy, the asterism of the Big Dipper is called Saptarishi, with the seven stars representing seven sages/seers. *Saptarishi*, in Hindu mythology, refers to the seven revered ancient sages or rishis who played a significant role in shaping the cosmic order. Also known as the wise Seven Seers, they are often identified as *Marichi, Atri, Angiras, Pulaha, Kratu, Pulastya, and Vashishtha.* The *Saptarishi* are considered eternal and are mentioned in various Hindu scriptures, including the *Vedas* and *Puranas*.

Dhruv*P71: In Hindu mythology, *Dhruv* is a legendary figure and a devotee known for his unwavering devotion to Lord *Vishnu.* As a child, *Dhruv* sought a permanent place in the cosmos and, blessed by *Vishnu*, became the pole star, symbolizing steadfastness and spiritual dedication.

Vishnu*P98: One of the principal deities in Hinduism, often re-garded as the preserver and protector of the universe. In the Hindu trinity, he is part of the triumvirate alongside *Brahma* (the creator) and *Shiva* (the destroyer). *Vishnu* is known for incarnating in various forms, or avatars, to restore cosmic order and uphold dharma (righteousness).

Kalpas*P100: In Hindu and Buddhist cosmology, a "*kalpa*" refers to a vast period of time, often representing the cycle of creation, duration, and dissolution of the universe. It's a concept used to describe immense time spans.

Adishesh*P100: Are considered as divine support or foundation for the universe. It represents the cosmic bed or resting place for Lord *Vishnu*, who is the preserver in the Hindu trinity. *Adishesha* (the primordial serpent) is known by various epithets such as, *Anantashesha, Sheshanaga.*

*River Ganges**P152:* The Ganges, often referred to as the *Ganga*, is a sacred river in India,. It holds immense religious significance in Hinduism and is considered to be purifying.

Diva or Diya**P115:* It is a significant symbol in Indian cultures. It is a small lamp usually made of clay/terracotta, with a cotton wick dipped in oil or ghee. When lit, the diya symbolizes the triumph of light over darkness and good over evil.

*Stygian or Styx**P142:* In Greek mythology, one of the rivers of the underworld. The word *styx* literally means "shuddering" and expresses loathing of death. In Homer's Iliad and Odyssey, the gods swear by the water of the *Styx* as their most binding oath.

*Ardhanarishvara**P148:* The *Ardhanari* form of *Shiva* is a manifestation of the concept of *Ardhanarishvara*, which means the "Lord whose half is a woman." This form symbolizes the unity and balance of masculine and feminine energies in the universe

*Shiva**P152:* is one of the principal deities in Hinduism, representing the aspects of destruction and transformation. In short, *Shiva* is the god of destruction in the Hindu trinity, alongside *Brahma* (creation) and *Vishnu* (preservation)

*Trishambhu, Shambhu**P152:* Is a term associated with Lord *Shiva* in Hindu mythology. The term is a combination of two Sanskrit words: *Tri* meaning three, and *Shambhu*, an epithet for Lord *Shiva*. Therefore, *Trishambhu* translates to "The Three-eyed One" or "He who has three eyes."

*The Pilkhan Tree**P163:* It holds an immense cultural importance in India, where it is often associated with rituals and traditions. Its large, spreading canopy provides ample shade, making it a favored spot for gatherings and prayers.

Many writers and poets from Delhi, India and other countries, occasionally gather under the peaceful environment of the *Pilkhan Tree* at distinguished Indian Scholar, author and academician, Prof. MalashriLal and Robey Lal's residence in New Delhi, India, for sharing writings, readings and gathering inspiration from each other. This unique group was initiated/cordinated by Prof. Alka Tyagi, a poet, writer and a scholar of *Kashmir Shaivism and Agam Shastra.*

Shesh-Shaiyya, Anant-Shaiyya**P100 *are* generally depicted with a massive form that floats coiled in space, or on the universal ocean, to form the bed on which *Vishnu* lies. Sometimes shown as five-headed or seven-headed, but more commonly as a many thousand-headed serpent, sometimes with each head wearing an ornate crown.

*Vānaprastha**P20: is a composite word with the roots *vana* meaning "*forest, distant land*", and *prastha* meaning "going to, abiding in, journey to". The composite word literally means "retiring to the forest". *Vanaprastha* refers to the third of four classically designed *ashrams (stages of life)* in Hinduism.

*Kaal*P86:* an age, era, or a particular point in time

*Rani Roopmati**P55: also known as Kavi Roopmati, was a poet queen of *Mandu**, central India and the consort of Sultan Baz Bahadur of Malwa. She is a central figure in Malwa's folklore, where tales often celebrate the romance between the Sultan and his beloved *Roopmati.*

*Saree*P127:* A garment consisting of a length of cotton or silk draped around the body, traditionally worn by women from Indian subcontinent.

Some excerpts from some past reviews

"In the crowded scene of loud feminist poets, she is a feminist who wants to celebrate the inner soul and capture the beauty of the female body. Every poem is accompanied by a sensual painting that is abstract to leap out of the mundane in search of ascension to nature." — *Yogesh Patel - The Book Review, February 2019*

"Meena Chopra's bold figurative work has self-assured certitude. But her abstract work is perhaps more interesting because it has a liminal quality. It's a reflection of her tenuous, hesitant, selfconscious process of freeing herself of creative excrescences and finding her core as an artist." —*Mayank Bhatt, Generally About Books, Aug 26. 2017*

"When Meena Chopra gazes at sunsets from the window of her Mississauga home, she's transported back to her childhood in northern India. For the internationally acclaimed poet and artist, it's inspiration that has filled countless pages and canvases with colourful words and images". —*Jim Wilkes, Toronto Star, Aug 09 2010*

"she often combines the two – Chopra's work focuses on the natural and abstractly emotional, showcasing a humanistic philosophy she also applies to her personal life". —*J.P. Antonacci, The Mississauga News, Mar 01, 2010*

The words and the visuals support each other and the viewer is taken on to a journey to the end of the clouds. Look at her art or read her poetry there is a feeling of scaling heights, going to the mist of the mountains and scenting the fragrant pines." —-*Nirupama Dutt, Indian Express (India), August 22 1999*

"Accompanying her paintings are her verses, and the two compliment each other. In Fact, they often seem to flow from and into each other, making one wonder which came first, the word or the image. The heightened passionate quality of her verses imbues the images with a strong emotional power"—*Manisha Vardhan , The Pioneer, New Delhi(India) August 11 1999*

-One notices a rhythm of universal duality underlying her poetry as well as her paintings. The poems strong in imagery and spontaneity complement the paintings" —*Critic , First City Magazine, January 1997*

"Images have been made use of in abundance while expressing her feelings, thoughts and views ..The poems are short but very powerful and impressive indeed! Meena strikes with force to show her caliber of thinking which is on par with any Indian modern poet who is of great repute. "-*M. Fakhruddin, Poets International, (India) December 1996*

"Her poems talk of 'hidden fire/rising with/a smoky thread...' A seemingly ordinary enough statement, it might also mirror the extraordinary sensibility of a committed artist."-*Adrian Khare, Blitz, Bombay, India 13.3 1993*

-One notices a rhythm of universal duality underlying her poetry as well as her paintings. The poems strong in imagery and spontaneity complement the paintings" —*Critic , First City Magazine, January 1997*

"Her poems have neat compactness of paintings; words become colours that fill up the canvas if-or when she is not using her brush. .. She is delicate but strong, gentle yet sharp, vulnerable yet proud. Self-actualization is more a matter of routine than effort; it is the moment beyond the ones of self knowledge that she wants to live up to, and become, not a mere rhapsody in search of life but a rhapsody in search of the deeper self. "—-*Gautam Siddharth, The Pioneer (Book reviews), Delhi, (India) 28.9.1996*

"A characteristic of her style is that physical sensations beauti-fully blend with abstract thought – yearning for fulfillment is attended upon by consciousness of fragmentation."—Dr. Shalini Sikka The Quest, (India) 1996

"In paintings there is a poetic beauty and poems are strong in imagery and spontaneity. And both types of work are intense in movement"—-*Deshbandhu Singh Rashtriya Sahara, Delhi, (India) August 1996*

Meena
Chopra

Biography of Meena Chopra:
A Fusion of Poetry and Visual Art

Meena Chopra, an internationally acclaimed poet, visual artist,
art educator, curator, and event producer, was born and raised
in the picturesque Himalayan hill resort of Nainital, India.
Since relocating to Canada in 2003, Meena has called Mississauga,
her home. Her artistic journey began in textile and garment
design, where she spent seven years as a lead designer with
renowned firms in New Delhi.

Later Meena continued to cultivate her creativity through poetry,
art, and sculpture while simultaneously exploring her entrepreneurial

spirit in marketing, advertising, and media. She started and ran an advertising agency in New Delhi, shifting from garment and textile designing career. She has been publishing an ethnic Entertainment and Art Newsweekly from Toronto. She also was running an afterschool education centre in Mississauga, Canada.

Meena has exhibited her art in premier galleries and museums across India, Canada, England, and the USA, amassing over 125 group and solo exhibitions. Her paintings, characterized by abstract beauty, find homes in collections of corporations, government bodies, embassies, hotels, and private collections worldwide.

Her artistic and poetic skills were honed under the guidance of master artists and poets in India. Meena has been professionally writing poetry since early nineties and creating visual art since 1985. Her work often blurs the lines between art and poetry, driven by the evocative power of abstract imagery. Since 2004, Meena has been actively curating, producing, and organizing multidisciplinary art exhibitions and events, most of them under the aegis of CROSS CURRENTS—Indo Canadian International Arts of which she was the founding president.

As a participating member of various art and literary groups in Mississauga and Toronto, Meena has made significant strides in the literary world, participating in readings and events across Canada and India. Her poetry performances often accompany her visual art, creating a harmonious blend of the two mediums.

Meena is an author of many art and poetry collections, and co-editor of an anthology. She is a bilingual writer, creating in both English and her native language, Hindi. Apart from her Hindi poems, Meena's poems in English and artworks have been published extensively in many prestigious literary, anthologies, journals and magazines. To name a few, *American Diversity Report, Poetry Pause by League of Canadian Poets, Word Fest by Mississauga Writers' Group, Canada Our Home*

*by Mississauga Writer's Group, Free Lit Magazine (Canada),
Artis Mag (Canada), Generally About Books (Canada), Indian
Voices(Canada), Word Masala (England), Poets International
(India), The Journal of the Poetry Society (India), Year Book
of Indian Poets 2023 (India) Capriccio (Germany) translation
Zenith (Austria) translation, Continuum by Poetry Club of India,
Setu Mag, Poets International, The Journal of the Poetry Society
(India), Silver years, Celebrating Time Travel and many others.
You can also find her poetry films created and produced by her
on her YouTube Channel.*

Her commitment and deep interest in collaborative artistic experiences
led her to become a qualified artist-educator from the Royal
Conservatory of Ontario. She advocates for the integration of
literary arts with other art forms, providing audiences with a
comprehensive artistic encounter. Passionate about cultural
diversity, Meena actively promotes different cultures through
art events. She taught arts to 'Special needs students at Learna
Education Centre and Pixie Blue Studio in Port Credit, Mississauga.
She held various art workshops throughout the Greater Toronto
Area. Meena continues to leave an enduring impact on the artistic
community, bringing cultures together through her unwavering
dedication to the visual and literary arts.

Her dedication to poetry and arts has earned her numerous accolades
and awards, including the Civic Award of Recognition from
the City of Mississauga for arts in 2022. Notably, she received
the 1st prize from 'Visual Arts Mississauga' in 2017 and recognition
from the National Ethnic Press Council of Canada for her
distinguished contributions to art and poetry. In 2003 She was
recognized for her poetry by the Mississauga Library System.
She also received the best Hindi Poet Nalanda Award in 2023.
She was awarded with the prestigious Mahadevi Verma International
Honour for her outstanding contribution to literature and arts
as a litterateur and artist of Indian origin residing outside India.
Among her many other accolades in community building,
Meena was honoured with the 'Outstanding Service and Commitment
to Diversity and Inclusiveness award' from Peel

Community Conections in 2006. Amongst other grants, The Canada Council for the Arts acknowledged her contributions with awarding her grant to represent Canada at an International Art Camp and Art exhibitions in Jaipur, India, in 2020 where twenty other countries had participated.

Amongst many other positions, she has been the Founder President and Director of CROSS CURRENTS – Indo Canadian International Arts, Past Secretary of Poetry Club of India, Past Chair of Carassauga Festival, Co-chair of Streetsville Arts Festival.

Email
artist.meenachopra@gmail.com

Website
https://www.meenachopra.art

Facebook ID
@meenachopra

Facebook Page
@meena.chopra.artist

LinkedIn
@choprameena

YouTube
@meenachopra

X
@meenachopra

Instagram
@meena_artist_author

Shadows crawl—
encircling the bodyline
grasping a restless streak.

Life breathes deep
Trembling with unformed desires
seeking freedom, unbound
entwining earth to sky——-

Meena
Chopra

https://youtube.com/shorts/uXkKWz5LXbg

DIGITAL PHOTO FRAMES LOADED WITH ORIGINAL ART VIDEOS AVAILABLE ON DEMAND

Digital Photo frames loaded with art videos are available on demand. Additionally, limited edition digital art prints on canvas, embedded with QR codes for video playback, can be ordered in various sizes from the author.

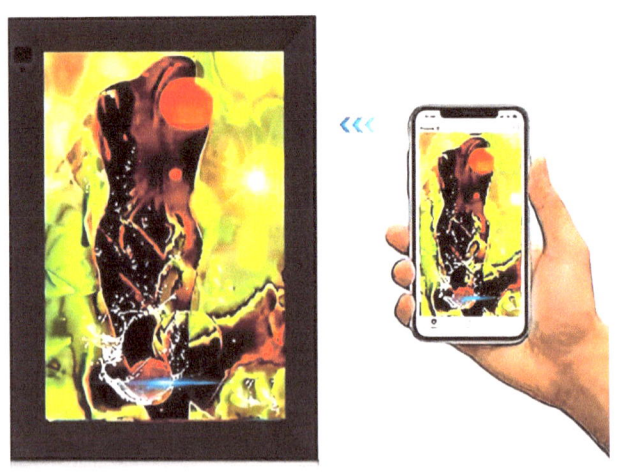